Peter Kocan was born in Newcast
and was raised in Melbourne. Afte
fourteen, he worked in country New

At the age of nineteen, Kocan wa   ﹍ ιοι the
attempted assassination of a Federal   ﹍ι﹍ιι. During the years
spent in penal and psychiatric institutions, he began writing
poetry and several collections of his poems have now been
published. His first novel, *The Treatment*, written after his release,
was published in 1980. Its sequel, *The Cure*, followed in 1983.

Since 1978 he has lived and worked on the central coast of
New South Wales. His hobbies include amateur theatre in which
he is involved as an actor and a playwright.

Also by Peter Kocan

PETER KOCAN

THE TREATMENT AND THE CURE

A&R Classics
An imprint of HarperCollins*Publishers*

A&R Classics
An imprint of HarperCollins*Publishers*, Australia

The Treatment first published in 1980
The Cure first published in 1983
Combined Sirius Quality Paperback edition 1984
This A&R Classics edition published in 2002
by HarperCollins*Publishers* Pty Limited
ABN 36 009 913 517
A member of the HarperCollins*Publishers* (Australia) Pty Limited Group
www.harpercollins.com.au

HarperCollins*Publishers*
25 Ryde Road, Pymble, Sydney NSW 2073, Australia
31 View Road, Glenfield, Auckland 10, New Zealand
77–85 Fulham Palace Road, London W6 8JB, United Kingdom
Hazelton Lanes, 55 Avenue Road, Suite 2900, Toronto, Ontario, M5R 3L2
and 1995 Markham Road, Scarborough, Ontario, M1B 5M8, Canada
10 East 53rd Street, New York NY 10022, USA

National Library of Australia Cataloguing-in-Publication data:

Kocan, Peter, 1947– .
The treatment; and, The cure.
ISBN 0 207 19900 0.
I. Title.
A823.3

Cover design: Russell Jeffery, HarperCollins Design Studio
Cover image: Coo-ee Historical Picture Library
Printed and bound in Australia by Griffin Press on 70gsm Bulky Book Ivory

7 6 5 4 3 2 1   02 03 04 05

Publisher's Preface

Since their sensational release in the early 1980s, Peter Kocan's two short novels, *The Treatment* and its sequel *The Cure*, have found enduring appeal with both critics and the public alike. Based on Peter's own experiences, the books examine a world few of us know or understand.

At the age of nineteen, Peter was given a life sentence for the attempted assassination of a Federal politician. He spent the following ten years in penal and psychiatric institutions, where he began writing in earnest.

The results of his labours were several volumes of poetry and the two novels, *The Treatment* and *The Cure*. The novels follow the fortunes of Len Tarbutt – also nineteen years old and serving a life sentence – through the trials and tribulations of gaol and a mental hospital. It is a harrowing and enlightening journey, one filled with much sadness and pain but also hope and humour. The writing is spare, compassionate and full of Peter Kocan's trademark wry wit – and, importantly, it transcends the decades, rendering the books as relevant and vivid today as when they were first published.

Sydney, 2002

THE TREATMENT

1

Down a long road all sun and shadowy with trees overhead and a slow look from cows across a fence and you're there. You see buildings with barred windows and a few people in old grey clothes. There's the Main Kitchen. There are trucks outside being loaded with steel dixies for the wards and a reek tells you that today must be stew or cabbage. Then you see a nurse in a blue dress leading a little flock of inmates beside the road. They're all small, like little boys or shrivelled old men, and are shambling and dribbling after her in a single file strung out for fifty yards. She turns and shouts for them to mind the car. One of them is right on the road. You see his face, all red and crumpled like a monkey's, coming closer through the windscreen. He's grinning. He likes the car, as though it's a big friendly animal coming to sniff him. Your driver toots, then stops.

"Johnny Bodley! Get off the road this instant!" the nurse shouts. When he doesn't move she walks back and takes him to one side. As you go past you can't help your eyes flickering over her legs and the swell of her chest. After the months at the gaol the sight stabs you. And now she might be the last woman you'll ever see.

The car gathers speed up around a winding curve past other ward buildings and you seem to be going away from the hospital again. There is dry scrub and yellow dirt with ant-mounds. Your stomach is watery with fear. Whatever you're going to is very close now. A high brick wall is just ahead. The car stops at an iron gate and the guard next to the driver presses a bell. A man in grey uniform comes out and unlocks, then holds the gate open.

"G'day," your driver says as we go through.

"G'day," the grey-uniformed man answers.

The car goes along a bit then stops outside a low sprawling building with barred windows. There is a door with an iron grid on the front. Your guards start to get out and motion for you to get out too. You'd rather not. It was so nice in the car, looking out the window, listening to the guards' small talk, knowing nothing much could happen to you until you got to where you were going. Now you'd got there.

There is a rattle of keys from inside and the door is opened by a grey-haired man in a grey uniform. Your guards exchange greetings with him while he unlocks the iron grid.

"How ya goin'?"

"Not bad. How's yerself?"

"Hot enough for ya?"

"Too bloody hot."

"Cool change due, they reckon."

"Yeah, hope so."

The talk has nothing to do with you. They seem to have forgotten you. We all step inside. The room is a pantry, with sinks and stainless steel and a big dishwashing machine and several dixies on a table. There are two more grey-uniformed men there, one of them wearing an apron, and three other men who must be inmates, also with aprons. They look at you and you don't know whether to look back or look away or what. You try to feel as though you belong with the guards, as though you're just one of a bunch of friends who've dropped by for a minute and will be going shortly.

The grey-haired man leads us down a corridor to an office. You catch a glance of a long verandah beyond a glass partition and several faces pressed against the glass, looking at you. For the first time the grey-haired man appears to notice you. He motions to a chair and you sit down. He is still talking with the guards and one of them is leaning over the desk, signing a paper. Then the grey-haired man signs a paper and the guard arranges it in a folder he carries.

"Well, we'd better get moving," the guard says. They all shake hands with the grey-haired man and move towards the corridor. You feel panic. You feel like begging them to take you back into the car to drive some more, even just for another hour. It was so good in the car, so safe, looking out the window, hearing the small talk, knowing nothing much could happen. As the guards go out they say goodbye. One of them gives a thumbs-up sign and says: "You'll be right, mate."

You grin at him and nod. You want to believe him. He was a good bloke. They were all good blokes. They know about these places and you tell yourself that you can believe what they say.

The grey-haired man comes back from seeing them down the corridor and sits at the desk. He arranges some papers in front of him. It's your file, the one the guards brought. You can see your name on the cover. The grey-haired man is looking at the file and also looking at you as though he's weighing you up.

"What's your name, lad?" he asks.

You are surprised. Surely he knows your name?

"Len, er, Len Tarbutt," you answer.

"How old are you?"

"Nineteen."

"Height?"

"Er, about five foot ten I think."

"What colour hair would you say you've got?"

"Um, blond I suppose."

"No, more brown I'd say."

You feel a clutch of apprehension. You feel you've said something wrong. That you'd been caught out in a lie, somehow. Then you realise that you haven't been calling him "Sir". That was enough to make them hit you, back at the gaol. Not calling them "Sir" was a Breach. You recall the time at the gaol when one of the men forgot to call the warder "Sir". The warder went up and put his arm round the man's shoulder, as if he felt very friendly, and said: "My friend, you know you've committed a Breach, don't you?" The man didn't really know. He probably didn't even realise about the "Sir". But he smiled and agreed. His mouth was trembling while he was smiling. Then the warder hit him in the face and he fell down.

The grey-haired man is looking at you. You're afraid he's thinking about the "Sir", or that you lied about your hair. Your throat feels so thick you can hardly speak.

"Um, my hair's blond when the sun shines on it, Sir." You realise how stupid that sounds and that he might think you're being insolent. Your heart is thumping. He looks at you for a while longer. Then he closes up the file.

"I think that'll be all for now," he says. "You can go out with the others."

He leads you out of the office and unlocks a door and you go through. You're on the long verandah. It's closed in with wire mesh on the open side and there are rows of benches set along the wall. There are a whole lot of men, some pacing up and down like at the gaol, some playing cards, some talking, some lying very still along the benches with little columns of smoke rising from their cigarettes. But the main thing you see is the view spread out in the distance. There is a big lake going right away for maybe two or three miles to a green haze of shore on the far side and green bush all around that comes right up to the high outer wall of this place. The ground slopes downwards from the verandah right down to the water so that you look clean over the top of the wall from here. It's beautiful, especially because you didn't expect anything like that. It's the sort of view that rich people have from their patio, except for the wire mesh. Outside the mesh is a yard about twenty feet wide. It's bounded at the edge by a mesh fence with barbed wire on top. Beyond that, and still sloping down, are vegetable gardens and then the main wall. To one side of the vegetable gardens is a lovely-looking tiled swimming pool, shining all white and blue and cool. The water is shimmering in the sunlight.

You stand gazing out over everything, partly because it's so beautiful and partly because you don't know what else to do. Some of the men are staring at you. You don't know whether to look back at them or not. Men at the gaol had warned you about these madhouse inmates.

If you offended them, or even if you didn't, they might suddenly attack you. Madmen have the strength of ten. That's what you heard anyway. While you're standing there a little dark man, one of the ones pacing up and down, bumps against you. He is staring straight ahead and muttering: "Shut-up, shut-up, shut-up, shut-up..." over and over. You edge away, pretending you haven't noticed him.

"Hey, Len!" someone calls. It's one of the men playing cards. You look carefully. You recognise a face. Bill Greene! You

6

suddenly feel much better. You knew Bill Greene only slightly at the gaol, but now you feel he's your long-lost brother.

"Hi Bill, how ya goin'?" you cry, overflowing with goodwill. Your brain's ticking now and you make a big show of greeting Bill so the other men will see you've got a mate here who'll probably back you up if anyone starts anything.

"Jeez, Bill, I didn't know you were here."

"Been 'ere two months."

"Yeah? What's it like?"

"Better than gaol, mate."

"Listen mate, what's the drum?"

You're feeling so relieved now that you almost laugh to hear yourself using terms like "What's the drum?". It's part of the hearty-matey pose you need to use at first, to show you're one of the blokes and not just some innocent kid. Someone might be sizing you up. Still, it sounds so funny you almost laugh.

"Give us the oil, mate," you say.

"Aw, there isn't much to it," Bill Greene says. "It's pretty easy really."

"What're the screws like?"

"Most of 'em are all right. There's a few cunts, though."

"What about biffings?"

"Pretty rare."

"Yeah? Dinky-di?"

"Yeah, they don't have to biff much. They've got other ways. Like shock treatment."

"Christ! What d'you have to do to get shock treatment?"

"Play up. Act mad. Anything really. It just depends on the screws and the doctor."

"Who's the doctor?"

"Ward doctor. He comes round every coupla days. He likes giving shock. 'Electric Ned' they call him."

"Real cunt, is he?"

"Aw, he's all right in some ways. He just likes giving shock whenever he can."

"Have you had it?"

"No, but I've come close a few times."

You're not feeling so cheerful now, with this talk of shock treatment. You start to think how it was all too good to be true. Now you're finding out about the bad thing, the thing you knew had to be here though you didn't know exactly what it would be. Shock treatment! It had a very bad ring to it. Especially the word "treatment". When they biffed you it was pretty bad, but at least you knew they were doing something they shouldn't be doing. They knew it too. There was always a chance they'd get into trouble for biffing. Not much of a chance, but a chance. Also, some screws didn't agree with biffing and they'd try to stop other screws who did it. But "treatment" was different … they could do it with a clean conscience because they were just trying to help you.

"Who's the grey-haired bloke in the office?" you ask Bill Greene.

"That's Arthur, the Charge Nurse."

"Is that what you call him? Arthur?"

"Yeah, you call the screws by their first names here."

So you go on talking to Bill Greene while he's playing euchre with three other inmates. And while you're looking around the verandah you start to recognise a few other faces you remember from the gaol. There's Nick, a little Italian. And Dave Lamming. And Barry Clarke who went to court the same day you did and got life for killing his girlfriend and shoving a broom-handle up her. Barry was famous at the gaol. His jury stayed out only nine minutes. That was supposed to be a record, at least for a murder. You think about saying hello to him, but he looks peculiar, shuffling along like a drunk man and his face all loose and his mouth dribbling.

"What's the matter with Barry Clarke?" you ask Bill.

"He's on medication. That's another thing here. They whack medication into you and some of it's pretty bad."

"What does it do to you?"

"Have a look at Barry."

"He's like a zombie."

"That's what it does. Shock does the same thing." You decide you'd like to change the subject.

"What do you actually *do* here?"

"Most of the blokes work in the vegetable garden. A few have jobs inside the ward. Pantry work. Stuff like that."

"Do you have a choice in what you do?"

"Sometimes you do. Just depends."

"What's the best job?"

"The gardening's all right. Gets you out in the open a bit. Inside jobs have more lurks—like pantry workers get extra food. Stuff like that."

Then you ask the question you've been waiting to ask.

"Does anyone ever, sort of, go berserk? Is there anyone you have to watch out for?"

"Aw, not really."

Bill's casual tone is very reassuring.

"You hear talk at the gaol about this place. They reckon blokes go berserk all the time, and how you have to be careful or you get your throat ripped out or something."

"That's mostly shit, mate. Someone might go off now and again, but nothing much."

So you let Bill Greene go on with his euchre while you sit and think about what he's told you. On the whole it doesn't sound too bad. Except for the shock treatment. Except for the medication. Those two things.

A screw calls out that lunch's ready and the inmates all get up and move toward the door of the dining room. You follow them into the room and see eight tables. The others sit down at their places and you stand waiting for someone to tell you where to sit. A screw waves you to a chair. There is a glass of orange juice and a spoon at each place. The dining room is connected to the pantry by a servery cut in the wall and you see somebody's hands pushing plates of food through. Three screws in aprons are taking the plates and bringing them to the tables like waiters. You feel uneasy about this, as though it's wrong for screws to be waiting on you. The food makes you uneasy too. It's so good, better than any gaol food, even the gaol food on Christmas Day when they give you a piece of plum duff with custard. You eat carefully, with your eyes down, as if you want to show that you understand the food is too good for the likes of you and that you don't deserve to be waited on and that you aren't gloating about it or anything.

There's a lot of noise coming from the pantry, laughing and yelling and banging of plates and dixies. The dining room is quieter with just the clink of spoons and eating noises. You're at a corner table with five other men who are all very messy with their food. They all look drugged. One of them is Barry Clarke and he can hardly eat. His mouth is slobbering and his tongue's poking out and getting in the way of the spoon and he is making a gurgling sound in his throat and spilling the food down his jacket. A screw keeps coming over to him.

"For Christ's sake Barry, don't be such a bloody pig."

He takes the spoon and tries to show Barry how to put it in his mouth, but as soon as he takes his hand away the spoon goes crooked against Barry's tongue and the food spills.

"Bloody sure you won't be invited to Government House!" the screw says.

Barry is mumbling something with his thick tongue. The screw takes a while to understand what he's saying. Barry wants to go for a piss.

"No, be buggered!" says the screw. "You can wait."

A minute later there is a trickling sound under the table and you feel your foot getting wet. Barry is pissing. You try to pull your foot back out of the way. The screw notices the piss and throws up his hands in disgust.

"Jeeeesus!" he says. He goes for a mop.

The rest of the afternoon you stand looking out through the verandah wire at the lake. Now that you're here, actually here, and you've seen and heard enough to make you think that maybe you'll survive all right, you start to remember the other thing, the Life sentence, and the hollowness comes back into your stomach. You're doing Life. That means seventeen or even twenty years in this State. Fifteen if you're very lucky. But that's when you're doing the time in gaol. Doing it here, well, who knows? Being here means you're Criminally Insane, a psychopath, and they don't let psychopaths out if they can help it. You look along the verandah and think that this is for fifteen or twenty years, or maybe until you're an old man. Just this verandah and the outside yard and the dining room and the vegetable garden stretching on for probably twenty years at least. You feel the way you did when you were a little kid lost in Woolworths big store and you just stood there crying until some kind lady bent down and asked you what the matter was and then took you by the hand and found your mummy for you. Then your mummy gave you a big hug and you cried some more, but differently, because the fright was over. But now there weren't any kind ladies and no mummy, and crying wouldn't help.

There are some men down in the vegetable gardens working with spades and mattocks. Some of them are bare to the waist and brown from the sun. They're working slowly, and you can hear the soft sound of the mattocks hitting the earth and a faint sound of the talking and sometimes a shout or a joke. Screws are standing around on the high ground watching the men, or strolling among them. One screw's listening to the mid-week races on a transistor radio. Across the wall, the lake is a different colour from before lunch, darker blue and all ruffled by a lovely breeze that you can feel on your face.

At three o'clock two pantry workers carry a big tea-urn and a tin of biscuits down to the garden workers, then come back and bring another urn and more biscuits out to the verandah. You line up with some other men for a cup of the tea and a biscuit. The tea has milk and sugar in it. You begin to feel cheerful again, thinking that, anyhow, this is better than gaol.

At six o'clock the men start gathering near two heavy doors at each end of the verandah where the cells are. All the screws are there with their bunches of keys. The men go through the doors and start undressing and putting on pyjamas. Each man has a little plastic cup of water and some of them have a book or magazine too. Then a screw leads each man to his cell and locks him in. Your cell is halfway down the row. It has pale yellow tiles on the walls and the floor is some kind of rubber. It has a bed and an open rubber tub like the gaol tubs for pissing in. You can shit in them too, but they're so small it's hard to squat over them properly, and the shit smell fills up the cell all night.

When everybody's locked up, the screws go away. You sit on your bed and look around the cell. It has a window with a sort of steel lattice over it. You can see the main wall a few yards away, and along to the left you can see part of the main gate. There's a rose bush growing under the window, but you can only see the top of it because of the angle of the sill. It's very quiet, with only a cough or squeak of bedsprings from the other cells. You can faintly hear a television set from another part of the ward where five men are sitting up till nine-thirty. You've been told about the roster for sitting up, and that you've been put on the roster for another night. All the cell lights are left on till the rostered men are locked in their cells. The light in your cell seems awfully bright, with the bare bulb over your head and the reflection from the yellow tiles. A low rhythmic sound of moving bedsprings comes from one of the cells.

"Hey Don!" a voice calls.

"What?" another answers.

"Stop fucking yer fist!"

"Get stuffed!"

After a while the night screws come down the row of cells, trying all the locks and looking through the narrow peephole in each door. You see an eye looking at you.

"G'day," the screw says.

"Hullo," you reply.

The eye disappears. From the window you can see the day screws going out with their kitbags and then hear the noise of cars driving away. It's very quiet again.

You stay at the window, watching the sky getting dark above the wall and the leaves of the rose bush jerking in the breeze. Then you think you'll try to sleep. You get into bed and pull the blanket up over your head to block out the light. You find it hard to breathe like that, so you try screwing your eyes shut tight instead, but the light is still bright through your eyelids. You try facing the wall, but the tiles are reflecting the bulb straight into your face. You lie there, trying to think of something. You think of the roll of toilet paper beside your tub. You could lay a few thicknesses of toilet paper across your eyes and maybe tie them behind your head so

12

they'll stay in place. You congratulate yourself on your brilliance, but then realise that the screws might think you are mad if they peep in and see you with toilet paper tied around your head. Shock treatment. Medication. No, you don't dare risk it. You toss and turn for what seems like hours, then you drift into sleep.

A loud banging wakes you up and daylight is in the cell. Your door is thrown open. Men are carrying their tubs outside to empty them at the lavatory on the verandah. You take yours out too, come back and make your bed, then get your clothes from the piles at the end of the corridor, and dress. You wash and shave with a locked razor at a row of basins on the verandah.

The morning is beautiful. The sky is hazy blue and the sun coming up from the other side of the lake makes the water like a sheet of blazing steel, so blinding you can only look at it for a moment. Birds are singing. The men are cheerful. Two of them are playing ping-pong and the sound of the ball going back and forth seems a bit like birdsong, only faster. There are several card games going and the players are slapping the cards down with great energy and talking and arguing loudly. Not all the men are active though. Some have gone back to lie on the benches they'd been stirred from the night before. The same little blue columns of cigarette smoke are rising from them again. There's a whirring sound coming from the television room where somebody's buffing the floor with an electric polisher. You have ten minutes walk up and down the verandah to stretch your muscles, falling into step with Bill Greene and Dave Lamming who're doing the same thing. Dave's a thin little timid man. He's worried. Yesterday he told the Charge he had a headache and asked for an Aspro. The Charge said he'd speak to the doctor about it. Bill Greene is disgusted.

"You'll never learn, Dave!" he says.

"It was a bad headache," Dave replies.

"Electric Ned'll give ya more than a bloody headache when Arthur tells him about it."

"I get my headaches a lot."

"Well, Electric Ned will say your headaches are really just a sign of mental distress and he'll whack some shock into you."

13

"I'll tell him I'm all right."

"He can't believe anything you say. You're mentally distressed."

"I'll ask Arthur if I can clean some windows," Dave says.

Cleaning windows is Dave's own therapy for when he's upset. Whenever you see Dave with a bucket and rag you know he's trying to soothe himself. Dave is very upset now. His voice is trembling.

"You don't really think they'll give me shock do you?" he asks Bill.

"Aw, probably not," Bill replies in a softened tone.

"D'you reckon they will, Len?" Dave asks you.

"Aw, probably not," you say. You've no idea really, but you hope they won't. You're telling yourself never to complain of a headache or ask for an Aspro. Be careful about windows too.

Breakfast is delicious. Orange juice, scrambled eggs, two slices of buttered bread. You're very hungry after the long night in the cell.

After breakfast the garden workers start putting on work-boots and wide hats. You're called to the Charge.

"How d'you fancy a bit of gardening?" he asks.

"I'd like it," you reply, having to check yourself from adding "Sir". You don't dare call him "Arthur" yet.

"Well, Grumps will give you some work gear."

Grumps is an old inmate who looks after the clothing store and does errands for the screws. He wears old tatty slippers and shuffles along swearing and moaning under his breath. You go with Grumps and he gets you a pair of boots and a straw hat. He takes a long time because he keeps stopping to swear and groan.

When you've put on the boots and the hat you go to join about twenty other men waiting at the verandah gate. Five or six screws are there and the senior screw unlocks the gate and you all go through into the outer yard. The screw unlocks another gate and you file through into the vegetable garden. The men amble over to a tin shed and another screw hands out spades, mattocks and hoes. Then they wander to various parts of the vegetable garden and start digging or hoeing or turning soil over.

You ask a screw where you're supposed to work. He points to a plot where another man is digging.

"You can help Zurka," he says.

Zurka is a Pole. You remember the name vaguely from the news a long time ago. He ran amok in a train with a butcher's chopper. Killed a couple of people. You don't remember much about it, just the name. You start digging beside him. It feels good, the strain on your muscles, the earth under your feet, the warm sun on you. After a while you're sweating and the drops are trickling down under your shirt. The soil is already warm and dry on top from the sun and it throws up little bursts of dust when you turn each spadeful over, but an inch or two down it's still damp. You work very hard for a while, to show the screws how willing you are, until you start to get very sore in your back and shoulders, and also in your hands from gripping the smooth spade handle.

"The new bloke's a goer," you hear a screw say. Then he calls out to you: "Don't bust yourself, mate!"

You grin back at him, wondering if he's being sarcastic. You have a breather and look around at the other men. None of them are working hard. They seem to be taking a minute's breather for every minute's work. You do the same, but cautiously, in case you overdo it and get into trouble for bludging. The breathers give you plenty of time to look around and listen to the birds. There are small brown darting birds like sparrows—finches, you think—that fly so close over your head you hear their wings, and magpies walking about on the turned soil as though they're inspecting the work, and other birds sitting in rows on the top of the wall, and lots of seagulls wheeling in bunches and crying out.

There's some talking among the men and among the screws who sit or stand around on high points keeping watch. Whenever there's a question about planting or watering or anything important about the work, the screws will call out to ask Mario what he thinks. Mario is a very dark Sicilian who used to be a market-gardener, and he's the unofficial foreman here. His English is very poor. He only has two phrases: "Issa good" and "Issa no good", so you have to ask him very simple questions.

"We water carrots? Yes?"

"Issa good!"

If Mario doesn't agree he shakes his head sadly as though he's in despair at such foolishness.

"We dig this bed, Mario?"

"Issa no good. Issa no good."

"We dig that one then?"

"Issa no good." More despair. More head shaking.

"What about this other one?"

"Ah, issa good!" Mario brightens up.

"Mario a cunt? Yes?"

Mario makes a rude Sicilian sign with his fingers.

At ten-thirty the morning tea and biscuits are brought down and we all lie on the grass around the urn for fifteen or twenty minutes. Sometimes, if there's an interesting conversation going on, we stay drinking tea and lying on the grass for half an hour. It's lovely lying there with a pleasant tiredness in your muscles and the sun on your face, listening to the talk. Then a screw will sigh wearily and say: "Ah well, boys, we'd better strike another blow or Arthur'll be after our balls," and the men get up slowly and go back to work. We stop work at eleven-thirty and hand our tools in at the tin shed. Anyone who wants a swim can go to the pool. Almost everyone does. There are piles of swimming trunks and towels and a big red ball to play with. For thirty minutes you float in the cool blue chlorinated water or join in a rough game of water-polo, or sunbake, hardly able to believe you're really in the madhouse you've heard such awful tales about.

Electric Ned comes round after a couple of days. He wants to see the new man.

"He's a bit absent-minded," Bill Greene tells you. "Once he asked old Tom Hawksworth how he was settling in. Tom had been here for twenty-two years."

This incident is famous here. If anyone asks you how you're settling in, you know they're having a joke.

Electric Ned wears thick glasses and a white coat. He comes up to you on the verandah and shakes your hand very politely.

"You're Mr Tarbutt then," he says.

"Yes, doctor."

"How are you settling in?"

"Very well, thanks." You get ready to grin, but he's quite serious.

"No problems?"

"No, doctor."

"Feeling all right?"

"Yes, doctor."

"Doing a bit of work around the place?"

"Yes, gardening, doctor."

"Fine."

He gives you a long look through the thick lenses and goes away into the office.

"He seems all right," you remark to Bill Greene. Your heart is still thumping. You wonder what he's doing in the office. Maybe ordering immediate treatment for you.

"Yeah, as long as you stay on the right side of him," Bill replies.

You're going to try. Christ, you're going to try!

It's almost nine o'clock and you've got your work gear on and you're waiting near the verandah gate with the other men. A screw comes down the verandah carrying a tray with a cloth over it. You can see things sticking out. A silver kidney tray and cotton wool and some short lengths of rubber hose about four inches long. There's an antiseptic smell. The screw goes into a small room at the end of the verandah. Then Dave Lamming comes down the verandah looking deathly afraid. A screw is walking beside him, holding him by the elbow, and the doctor and Arthur are coming behind. As Dave goes past you turn your eyes away, as though there's something terribly interesting on the far side of the lake. Dave and the doctor and Arthur go into the small room after the screw. There is silence for a couple of minutes and then you hear Dave yelling: "I don't want it! Please! I'm all right! Oh please don't! Oh please! Oh please!" There is a sound of struggling. You hear screws' voices: "Don't be such a bloody kid, Dave!" and "The doctor knows what's best!" and "Hold his arms!" and other things.

Then there's a sudden buzzing sound and a choking and gargling, then silence. Your stomach is watery and you're shaking.

"Poor little bastard," says one of the men.

"He'll need Aspros now," says Bill Greene.

A screw comes to unlock the gate.

"Come on," he says, "it's not a friggin' side-show!"

You go down into the garden with the others and start digging. You work steadily, not daring to take a breather much. You want to show what a good inmate, a model inmate, you are. Dedicated. Eager to please. Then you get afraid you might be giving a wrong impression. You might be overdoing it. Showing "Obsessional Tendencies". Digging too much might be like cleaning windows too much. Two screws are sitting on a knoll a little way behind you. You imagine what they might be saying:

"Tarbutt's going pretty hard."

"Yeah, I noticed."

"Seems agitated."

"Better mention it to the doctor."

So you slow down and take a lot of breathers. Then you get afraid again. You wonder what the screws are saying. Maybe:

"Tarbutt seems a bit lethargic."

"He was going like steam a minute ago."

"Yeah, he's very erratic, isn't he."

"We'd better mention it."

So you work a bit faster, but not too fast, or too slow. You're concentrating so hard on timing every move to what you think is a proper balance between fast and slow that you feel giddy. You imagine what the screws might think if you fell over:

"Tarbutt fell over."

"Yeah, for no apparent reason."

"Peculiar."

"We'll have to report it."

You try to steady yourself. You take deep breaths. You're sure the screws are watching you and talking about you and you feel a wild urge to go up to them and assure them that you're not mentally disturbed or anything like that. You imagine how it would go:

"Er, I was wondering if you've noticed anything odd about my behaviour?" you might say.

"How d'you mean, Len?"

"I mean … well … whether you think I'm mentally disturbed."

"Why should we think that?"

"Because of the way I was working."

"What about the way you were working?"

"Well, fast and then slow."

"Why were you working like that?"

"I was a bit, sort of worried about how it might look. I mean, I wasn't worried, I was just thinking how it might look to anyone who was watching me."

"Do you think someone's watching you?"

"Well, no, I mean, not really. I mean, I'm not worried about it."

"You seem worried."

"No."

By now you know that you've made things much worse. You've delivered yourself to that small room at the end of the verandah.

"Tell us about this person you think is watching you."

"I don't think anyone is watching me."

"You said someone or something is watching you."

"No."

"Do you hear this person's voice when he's watching you?"

"No."

"He just watches you."

"Nobody watches me."

"That's not what you said a minute ago. Is it?"

"No."

"This creature or whatever it is, can you see him?"

"There isn't any creature."

"So he's a person then? A human?"

"No."

"A sort of spirit?"

"Look, he's nothing!"

19

"A sort of nothingness that watches you?"

"There's nothing there at all!"

"Does this nothingness ever try to harm you? Does he tell you to do things?"

"Do what things?"

"You tell us, we want to help you."

"Christ! You're twisting everything around!"

"Don't get upset, Len."

"I can't help getting upset when you twist things."

"Is that what the nothingness tells you? That we're twisting things? That we're trying to harm you?"

"I don't think you're trying to harm me at all."

"You said we're twisting things."

"I just mean that you've got it wrong."

"We're trying to understand, Len. We really are. If you tell us about this nothingness, this spirit or whatever it is, we'll be able to understand better."

"Can't we just forget the whole thing?"

"No, Len, we can't. This belief of yours about the Nothingness Spirit is obviously making you very distressed and unhappy."

"There isn't any Nothingness Spirit! Please believe me!"

"But you just told us about it."

"I didn't!"

"Well, how would we know about it if you didn't tell us."

"You just invented it."

"No, it's something in your own mind, Len."

"My mind's all right. Honestly."

"Do you know what this place is, Len?"

"Of course I do."

"What is it?"

"A psychiatric hospital."

"That's right. And why do people come to psychiatric hospitals?"

"Because of mental problems."

"Right. And you're here, aren't you?"

"Yes, but my mind's all right."

"Are you saying you're being held unjustly?"

"No, I wouldn't say that."

"So, you admit that you need treatment?"

"I suppose so."

"That's fine. It shows you have what's called 'insight'. You've done the right thing by telling us about the Nothingness Spirit. We'll tell the doctor all about it and he'll be able to help you. Any time the Nothingness Spirit starts to bother you, you let us know. Will you do that?"

"Yes," you say, defeated, knowing you've destroyed yourself. Knowing that within an hour the Nothingness Spirit will become a reality in your file. A true presence in cold print on the page. A living force that will be summoned by other minds to explain every sleepless night, every change of mood, every odd remark, every laugh, every tear, and every facial expression you will wear for the rest of your life.

You have created your own demon.

You know it would go something like that. Even if the details are wrong, it would go something like that. So you can't say anything to the two screws who are probably watching you. You struggle to calm yourself. You take deep breaths. You have a breather and stare away to the blue haze of the sky with your eyes half shut against the sun and try to think the sky down into yourself. The sky is so very calm and old and has seen more troubles than your own. You suddenly remember some words: "Yea, though I walk through the valley of the shadow of death, I will fear no evil: for Thou art with me."

Lovely words. They give you a feeling you can face whatever might happen. You're not religious. You've never been to church. You suppose the words are something about God, but it's the words themselves, and the strong, gentle sound of them, and the picture they give you that suddenly makes you feel all right, or nearly all right. They must have been written thousands of years ago, yet it's as though they're meant for you, yourself, right now. You let out a deep breath and there's a sort of good tightness in your chest and you don't feel very afraid of the two screws talking, or about digging fast and slow, or even about the room at the end of the verandah.

***

It's Thursday, the night you're rostered to sit up watching television. At six o'clock, when the other men are going into their cells, you go into the television room with the four who are rostered with you and the screws lock the door behind you. There's a billiard table in the middle of the room and the television set is up on a high stand near the window. The five of you move your chairs into position near the billiard table so you can rest your feet on the side of it if you want to. Or you can pull two chairs together to make a couch and lie full length. There's Bill Greene and Ray Hoad and Zurka and another man named Williamson, whom they call The Wild Man as a joke because he's so timid. The Wild Man has got a brass whistle and a cigarette lighter the screws gave him. It's forbidden to take your own matches or lighter into the television room at night, so they let The Wild Man have an official lighter for the five men. Nobody uses it. They all bring their own lights anyway. The whistle is to call the screws from the office if anyone goes berserk or anything. The Wild Man is very embarrassed about having the whistle.

"Blow yer whistle, mate," Bill Greene says to him.

The Wild Man grins, very sheepishly.

"Give it a blast. Go on," says Ray Hoad.

"No, it's all right," says The Wild Man.

"You'd better test it," says Ray Hoad. "The pea might've fell out."

"I heard something drop," says Bill Greene.

"Jesus, The Wild Man's lost his pea!" cries Ray Hoad.

"He'll be buggered without it," says Bill Greene.

"Sure it's not in yer pocket?" says Ray Hoad.

"Turn 'em out," says Bill Greene. He starts helping to turn out The Wild Man's pockets.

"That pea's government property!" says Ray Hoad.

"The whistle won't work without it," says Bill Greene.

"What if somebody goes berserk?" says Ray Hoad.

"There'll be murder done!" says Bill Greene.

"Blood all over the room!" says Ray Hoad.

"They'll probably tear The Wild Man to bits!"

"It's his own fault. Won't keep his bloody whistle in workin' order."

They both look solemnly at The Wild Man.

"Yer in a tight corner, mate."

"Up shit creek!"

"Without a paddle."

Bill and Ray make a show of conferring together.

"D'you reckon we can do anything?"

"We'll do what we can."

"But we can't promise anything."

"No."

"We might be able to save him from gettin' killed."

"Just depends."

"He might get hurt pretty bad."

"Luck of the game."

"He's not a bad sort of a bloke."

"Good fella."

"Except for his temper."

"I forgot about that."

"Ya can't hold him when he gets goin'."

"He goes berserk."

"He might go off any minute."

"Look at his face."

"It's turnin' savage."

"Blow the whistle, mate."

"Can't. The fuckin' pea's lost!"

The Wild Man is still grinning. Sheepish. He's used to this. There's a musical show on, and a beautiful girl is singing "Help Me Make it Through the Night". The camera is right up on her face and lips and you can see the little throbbing pulse in her throat when she sings the long notes, and when the camera draws back, you see the swell of breasts out of her dress and then her leg through a slit at the side. The men are all quiet, watching, not wanting the song to stop.

You're not thinking about sex, exactly, but about something more, something harder to put into words, as though the girl isn't just one girl, but all the girls and women in the world wrapped into herself. You keep your eyes on her until the song's finished and then you realise you're feeling miserable all of a sudden. A drama show comes on, with police cars and sirens and a lot of punching and chasing up fire escapes. It seems stupid. You stand looking out of the window at the dark night. There are some trees being blown by the wind. If you listen carefully when the television goes quiet for a moment you can hear the chain of the main gate clanking whenever a big gust comes.

At eight o'clock the two night screws come in with the tea-urn. One of them is called Eddie. He's got a sharp face and a way of sneering when he speaks. His favourite word is "fuck", but he pronounces it "faaark", like the cry of a crow.

"Faaark, you blokes have it easy," Eddie says to us. "Nobody brings me a cuppa, not even me faaarkin missus."

"Well, you wouldn't be bringin' us one either if it wasn't in the regulations," says Ray Hoad. Ray isn't afraid of screws.

"Faaarkin oath I wouldn't!" says Eddie. "If I was in control I'd have all you faaarkin blokes put down."

"Thousands 'ud agree with ya," says Ray Hoad.

"That's faaarkin right. Why should the taxpayers be keepin' you cunts in food and clothes?"

"If it wasn't for us, you'd be out of a job."

"Don't faaarkin kid yerself!"

Everyone is pretending that this is just a bit of friendly banter.

"Hitler had the right faaarkin idea. Crims, pervs, poofters, all into the faaarkin oven."

"What about morons?" says Bill Greene, looking directly at Eddie.

"Faaarkin morons too!"

Eddie and the other screw go out and lock the door behind them.

"Faaark. Faaark. Faaark," croaks Bill Greene, flapping his elbows like a giant crow. Then he farts loudly.

At nine-thirty we're put to bed. After the screws have gone and everything is quiet, you lie listening to the wind. The moon is near the top of your window and throws a silver sheen against the foot of the bed. You sleep for a while. Then you are awake and someone is shouting from one of the cells. George Pratt is yelling that the "Sallies" are after him. He's got an obsession about the Salvation Army, and often shouts in the night like this. Voices from other cells are telling him to shut up. Then you hear the screws in the corridor, and Eddie's voice.

"Shut yer faaarkin noise or I'll give yer a faaarkin needle in yer faaarkin bum!"

George Pratt's yells fade to low sobbing and you go back to sleep.

2

You've been here a few weeks now.

It's hard sometimes, having to go into your cell at six o'clock every night, especially on hot stuffy nights when the walls seem to press in on you and you know you won't be able to sleep for hours yet and you don't feel like reading. You can stand at your window and look out at the patch of grass and wall and the dulling edge of sky above the wall, but you've stared at them so often and so long that they seem to be closing in on you too, just like the cell. At times you feel so closed in you almost panic and have to get a grip on yourself. And when you've got your panic under control a little and are feeling better, you realise you've only been in the cell for maybe an hour and there are more hours to go before you'll be able to sleep, then you get panicky again. All you can do is lie on your bed, with your face turned away from the light and think, except that you don't want to think too much.

The cell is about the same size as the little rented room you had when you were free. You lie thinking about the last night in that room, when you were preparing to do the thing that you got the Life Sentence for.

You were sawing the barrel from a .22 rifle. The hacksaw blade was too light for gunmetal and kept bending and warping. You were also worried about the noise of it. The walls were very thin and you were afraid the men in the other rooms might get suspicious. They might even be spying through some crack or peephole, though you'd often examined the walls for openings and could find none. Still, you couldn't be sure, and the thought bothered you, especially whenever you masturbated.

When the barrel was off you began sawing the stock, halting every few seconds to listen. The stock came away after a long time. You put the sawn off pieces in the bottom of your wardrobe and then sat looking at the gun. It was small and neat, yet somehow larger than itself, as though huge forces lay inside it. You imagined it displayed one day in a glass case with a printed card describing what it had done.

For a long time you stood posing with the gun in front of the dressing table mirror, striking attitudes, experimenting with angles and postures. It was a new self you saw: the set of the shoulder, the curve of the cheekbone, the elbow cradling the gun, all seemed suddenly significant. You felt a kind of hum coming from inside yourself, like the hum of a live bomb.

You were thinking, again, about the problem of the photograph. It seemed impossible. You'd wanted to leave a picture of yourself where the police and reporters could find it; one showing you at just the right angle, with the gun held just so, and a smile on your lips. The smile was important. You weren't a glowering maniac, but a young instrument of fate. A blond death bringer. Your smile, frozen forever on the photo, would symbolise the poignant tragedy of everything. The picture mustn't look posed, though, more like a lucky accident that future historians would be grateful for. But how to do it? You couldn't ask anyone to photograph you. You knew nobody. Besides, the gun would cause alarm. For weeks you thought you'd had the answer—you'd take a photo of yourself in the mirror: then you realised you'd only get a picture of yourself taking a picture. You weren't stupid, exactly; it was just that your mind ran into blind alleys like that. Now it was too late to arrange anything. You didn't have a camera nor any money to buy one. The last of your money had gone on the gun.

You'd put the gun back into the brown paper wrapping and into the old carry-bag with the box of bullets. You thought vaguely of trying to tidy up the room. The police and reporters would be coming here and you wanted to make the right impression. Some things would have to be got rid of, such as the pile of girlie magazines. They weren't part of the image. The police and reporters would snigger and think you were one of those men who can't get a girlfriend. They wouldn't understand how you had *chosen* to live without girls and all that stuff. Had chosen the harsh road of destiny. They'd just think you were inadequate.

You began to feel that sweaty, nervous arousal that always came on you when you'd been thinking too long and too hard.

All day you'd been preoccupied with the gun and the plans and now your mind was starting to race and whirl, like an epileptic's brain when a fit is coming. Masturbation was the best thing then, because it made you calm afterwards and stopped the racing and whirling in your head.

You sat pondering the problem of Mrs Cassidy's bra again. Mrs Cassidy was the landlady. A big, talkative woman with floppy breasts that swung and wobbled inside her blouse. She hung her washing, including underwear, on the clothesline near the door of your room. You wanted to steal her bra and masturbate with it. It would be tricky. You'd have to do it under cover of darkness. You could keep the bra until just before dawn and then return it to the line. It made you terribly excited, thinking what you could do with Mrs Cassidy's bra. You could ejaculate into the cups. The sperm would dry and probably be unnoticeable against the white of the fabric. Mrs Cassidy might then wear it, actually wear your dried sperm against her nipples! You got a big horn just imagining it.

You opened the door and looked out into the yard to where the bra dangled almost within reach. Your heart hammered loudly. Then, as always, you got scared at the last moment. Perhaps the bra had been set as a trap. Everyone in the house thought you peculiar. They might have a system for keeping you under surveillance, watching the clothesline day and night. No, you weren't going to fall for it.

Mrs Cassidy cleaned your room every day. You would rather she didn't, but she just barged in with her own key when you were at work. For that reason, you kept the girlie magazines locked in the wardrobe. She, too, would misunderstand about them. Once, though, you'd deliberately left them out where she'd see them, excited by the thought of what her thoughts might be. Seeing the magazines, she might visualise you masturbating, naked and sweating on the bed. Many times since then you'd masturbated over your own mental picture of her mental picture of yourself.

All that was safe, or as safe as anything sexual could be. As long as you never actually showed sexual feelings to anyone you could feel in control of the situation. Even leaving the magazines for Mrs Cassidy to see was fairly safe. Even if she did have the thoughts you imagined her having, she'd blame her own dirty mind and you wouldn't be implicated. In your dealings with Mrs Cassidy, and everyone else, you came across as a polite, aloof young man with important things on his mind. Sometimes Mrs Cassidy and her male lodgers sat drinking beer in the kitchen, laughing and joking for hours. They'd invited you to join them at the beginning. Of course you never did. You were too shrewd to be caught like that. They never asked you again.

At work, too, you kept apart. The noise of the machinery in the factory was maddening, but at least it prevented conversation. At smoko and lunchtime, when the other men sat outside against the wall and talked about cars and football and sex, you always went down the street and sat in a quiet spot by yourself where you could think your own thoughts. That was the great thing, to be able to think, and you couldn't do it with people around. Sometimes you felt as if you had hardly any body at all, just thoughts. There were even moments when you'd suddenly become aware of your body ... a hand ... a foot ... and been astounded that you were an actual person with flesh and hair.

Now you hadn't been to work for several days. There wasn't any point.

The sexual arousal had gone. You sat staring around the room. You thought again of tidying up, but it seemed too much trouble. Torn butts of cinema tickets lay on the floor. Films were your only luxury and you spent most of your money on them. In a cinema you could float out of yourself into the bodyless world of feeling on the screen. To stop being yourself was lovely, it was happiness. Films had one terrible drawback though . . . they came to an end. The lights always came on and the real world was there waiting.

Last night you'd seen "Dr Zhivago" for the seventh time and the return afterwards had been very bad. The final scene, where Lara walks out into the street under huge portraits of Lenin and Stalin, to disappear forever, "a nameless number on a list afterwards mislaid", had filled you with a sort of ecstasy of grief.

You wanted to explode, literally, like a skyrocket, into nothingness. That was feeling, pure, untouchable, and you'd gladly have died right there in the seat rather than return to yourself and face the street outside with its squalor of traffic and people.

On the bus ride home you tried to keep that scene unspoiled in your mind, staring straight ahead with blank eyes like a shellshock victim, and whispering "Lara, Lara" under your breath. It was no use. The conductor came for the fare. Then a fat man sat beside you. The dirt on the floor and the traffic and the grinding of the bus's gears and the press of the fat man crept steadily through your consciousness until Lara was completely gone and all beauty and feeling with her. You were just yourself again, a shabby youth on a dirty bus. You knew it couldn't continue.

Dave Lamming has been getting shocks almost every day. He's had ten now and is like a zombie. He can't talk, or eat, or control his bowels, and the mess in his trousers stinks very much. His eyes are vacant and stare straight ahead, and if you try to talk to him, he'll just stare at you and maybe smile in a strange way, as if he half understands what you're saying, but he doesn't really understand anything, not even his own name. About four or five days after the last shock he starts coming out of the zombie state and then he's just very confused and can't remember anything. He doesn't know where he is.

"What's this place?" he keeps asking. A hundred times a day. "What's this place?"

"The railway station," Ray Hoad tells him.

"Is the train coming?" Dave wants to know.

"Yeah, any minute now."

So Dave sits patiently on the verandah, waiting for the train. Then he gets anxious.

"Why doesn't it come?" he asks.

"Won't be long," says Ray Hoad. Ray even tries to sell him a ticket. After another few minutes Dave has forgotten that this is the railway station.

"What's this place?"

"The surgical ward," says Ray Hoad. "You've just had your appendix out. It was touch and go. Complications set in." Dave feels his abdomen.

"You'll have a whopping bill to pay, mate," says Ray Hoad. Dave feels his pockets.

"I'm broke," he confesses. "I can't pay."

He goes to the office to tell them he can't pay the bill for his appendix. Electric Ned is there with Arthur. Through the glass partition we see Dave waving his hands and talking. We feel the joke's gone too far. Electric Ned and Arthur are looking our way. They know someone's been having fun with Dave. You drift into the background, away from Ray Hoad. Ray's not worried though. Ray Hoad isn't bothered by anything. He's our best at sport too.

There's a rough little field between the ward and the main gate, and at weekends the screws take us out to play cricket in the summer, or soccer if it's winter. It's lovely out there on a fine afternoon, the sky very clear with maybe just a few wisps of white cloud floating up high and the leaves of the trees touched with sunlight at their edges, so that if a breeze stirs them you get a beautiful, slow flash of golden light through the whole tree. The grass on the field is thin and tough and there are bare patches of brown dirt. When someone runs across and scuffs the bare patches it kicks up a small cloud of dust that catches the sun. If enough people are running about and scuffing the bare patches, you seem to be looking through a haze of dusty light across the whole field. The knock of the bat against the cricket ball makes a good sound, dry and solid, and makes you feel good somehow because that sound means that the bat has caught the ball cleanly in the centre and the ball is racing along the ground very fast. If the ball reaches the main wall it's worth two runs, or if it goes down under the trees it's worth two also. It's best when it goes down to the trees when you're fielding and you can run down after it and hurl it back with a big throw and then stay near the trees for a minute, looking up through the leaves with the brightness and shadow of them on your face. Sometimes the ball is hit right over the wall and a screw has to unlock the gate and go outside to find it in the scrub, and while you're waiting you can lie down on the ground, or roll a smoke, or just stroll about and think your thoughts.

The ball's over the wall now and we're waiting for the screw. There's Horse McCulloch sitting cross-legged in some long grass. He's called Horse because he's small and barrel-bellied like a Shetland pony and has a sandy coloured forelock. He's talking to Geoffrey Cleary who got four years for being a peeping Tom. Geoffrey is talking about how it felt in court.

"Were the women in the court?" Horse wants to know.

"Yeah, they had to testify."

"What sort of things did they say?"

"They told how they saw me sneaking outside the windows and stuff like that."

"What else?"

"Whether I had a horn or not."

"Fair dinkum?" Horse is excited.

"Yeah. The charge is more serious if you had a horn while you were looking in the window."

"Did you have a horn?"

"Not every time. I had one in court though."

The ball has come back. Clarrie Morton is batting. Clarrie used to be a boxer in the tent shows, and his nose and ears and eyes and mouth are all bruised out of shape. His mind's out of shape too from so many punches. Sometimes he thinks he's a cowboy film star called Dan Bunyip with a clever white stallion named Alligator. Or that he's Tony Palomino, a famous crooner that girls faint over. But now he's batting and doesn't think he's anyone. His reflexes are all wrong and he can't hit the ball at all. He's getting angry and very red with effort. After he's missed the ball ten or twelve times he grabs the bat by its blade and stares at the writing on it.

"No wonder this bat's no bloody good," he yells. "It's made of English willow!"

"Christ, no!" says Ray Hoad. He's shocked at the news.

Everyone gathers around the bat to look at the writing.

"Clarrie's right! It's English willow!"

"I'll be buggered!"

"Shockin'!"

"We can't play with this!"

"We need a proper cement bat!"

The cry goes up for a replacement bat. A proper cement one. One of the screws pretends to run back to the ward. Everyone is shaking their heads and clicking their tongues over the worthless bat. The screw comes back to say there isn't a cement bat to be had.

"Well, this is a fuckin' nice how-do-you-do!"

"A bloody disgrace!"

"What'll we do?"

"We'll just have to use the willow bat."

"Yeah, s'pose so."

"Nothin' else we can do."

So the game goes on and Clarrie is bowled out. But he doesn't feel so bad now because everyone knows it's the bat's fault.

3

"You've got a visitor," a screw tells you.

You go into the dining room, which is also the visiting room, and your mother is there. She looks towards you with her face very pale. She's looking you up and down, seeing if you're all right, not hurt or anything.

"Hello mum."

"Hullo dear," she says. "How's everything? Are you all right?"

"Yes mum."

"You look thin. Are you getting enough to eat?"

"Yes mum."

You sit down across the table from her. There's a long silence. A screw comes in and sits down at a far table and pretends to read his newspaper. The newspaper is partly to show that he's not really listening. You can't read a newspaper if you're listening. He sits half turned from your direction to let you know that he's a good fellow and isn't really going to watch you with your visitor, but he's still got you in the line of sight from the corner of his eye.

"How was your trip?" you ask your mother.

"Oh, not too bad," she says. "The train was a bit late getting away, that's all."

"Well, as long as the trip wasn't too bad," you say.

"No, it wasn't too bad."

"That's good."

Another long silence. For weeks you've been looking forward to a visit, now you can't think of much to talk about.

"I've baked you a cake," she says, suddenly fumbling in her bag. The screw is glancing across. Your mother brings out the cake. It's wrapped in cellophane.

"It's a fruit cake. You like fruit cake, don't you?"

"Yes, thanks."

"I'm afraid it didn't rise as well as it should have."

"It'll be fine."

"Would you like a piece now?"

"Er, no thanks, I'll have some later."

"It's got plenty of fruit in it. Dates, raisins and currants."

"Beaut."

More silence. You feel a tightness in your chest as though you're starting to suffocate. You're trying to think of something to talk about. The trouble is, you can only think about your life here, and you don't want to talk to your mother about that. You don't want to bring it out into the open about what this place is and why you're here. You want to keep the madness thing in the background because you know it would embarrass you both.

Your mother looks miserable. She's waiting for you to say something. To show you're truly glad to see her. You feel a stab of pain and pity for her. Your little mother, sitting there miserable because she loves you. She made you a cake and came all this way in the train to see you, and now you're sitting across the table like a stranger.

"What are the doctors like, dear? Do they seem nice?" she says. You both feel a little wince at the word "doctors", because mentioning "doctors" brings the madness thing a little into the open.

"We've only got one doctor. They call him Electric Ned."

"Why is that?"

"He likes giving shock treatment."

There's another wince at the words "shock treatment". "Shock treatment" is bringing the madness thing too close. You're both embarrassed now.

"Poor Auntie Janet had another stroke," she says to steer the talk away.

"That's a shame," you say. You only met Auntie Janet once, when you were a little boy. Even then, she was about eighty and smelled funny and you didn't like her. But now you want to talk about Auntie Janet.

"She must be pretty old now," you say.

"Over ninety," your mother says.

You try to think of something more to say about Auntie Janet. You can't.

"How's the weather been in the city?" you ask.

"Oh, reasonable. We had a light shower yesterday."

"Oh."

"How's it been up here?"

"Not too bad."

"That's good."

The silences are so awkward now you feel driven to ask a question it's probably better you didn't ask.

"Er, have you seen Stanislav lately?"

"I saw him about two weeks ago. He came into the bar while I was working. He was drunk of course."

"What happened?"

"Oh, he made a scene. The publican told him to get out and threatened to call the police. You can imagine what it was like."

Yes, you can imagine. In your memory stretches a dark series of scenes. Your stepfather drunk and violent, your mother crouched against the wall shielding her head with her hands and screaming for you to run for the police. You can't even calculate the number of times you ran in your pyjamas to the police station, only to be left loitering in the lobby while the policemen drank another cup of tea before setting out to deal with another "domestic". You remember the times you were brought home from the police station, trotting to keep pace with some tall silent constable who held your hand.

"What if mum's dead?" you used to ask yourself, plucking the question out of a whirl of half formed terrors. You wondered if the policeman would take you back to the station, to remain in the lobby in pyjamas, an orphan, until you grew up. There was always the same scene when you got back to the house; the policeman standing calm and disinterested in the hallway, while angry man and distraught woman made long and involved accusations against each other. Then the policeman would say that he wasn't going to take sides, but that there'd better not be any more disturbance.

Sometimes, when the policeman had gone, Stanislav gave your mother a few more hits around the face, but mostly he just called her some names that you didn't exactly understand and then he stormed out of the house. It was then, when the house was quiet again and you were tucked up in bed, that you began sobbing and trembling and sometimes vomiting. Then your mother would come in and clutch you to her bruised face and tell you about the "fresh start" that the two of you would make someday.

There's somebody swearing loudly outside on the verandah.

"Hey, cut the language," you hear Bill Greene's voice saying. "There's a visitor inside."

"Yeah, watch the faaarkin language," you hear Eddie add.

Your mother pretends she hasn't heard.

"What are the other ... er, men, like?" She was going to say "patients" or "inmates", but remembered about the madness thing.

"Most of them are all right," you say. Just then, Zurka comes in to say something to the screw. You call him to meet your mother.

"Er, mum, this is Zurka. He's one of the chaps I work with."

"How are you?" she says to Zurka. She's putting on a bright voice.

"Very well, thanks," he says. "How are you?" Zurka's Polish accent isn't very noticeable. You invite him to sit down, hoping he'll help keep the talk going and take some of the pressure off you. He sits down and talks to your mother about the weather and the gardening work and about her train trip. His manner is calm and easy, but you feel a faint worry when the talk is about the train trip. Zurka chopped those people up on a train and you're afraid the subject of trains might be risky. You're also feeling a vague sense of satisfaction to think that you can introduce your visitor to someone who's chopped people up.

Zurka is pleased to be able to talk polite small talk with an outsider. It's good practice for the future. He's been a model patient here for eleven years and the rumour is that he'll soon be transferred to the other section of the hospital where he'll be in an unconfined ward. If you get sent to an unconfined ward, it means the authorities are planning to set you free after another four or five years maybe.

Your mother's telling him about her work as a barmaid, and about how it's hard on the feet, standing pulling beers all day.

"I worked as a cellar man once," Zurka says.

"Oh, which hotel?" your mother asks.

"The White Crown."

"I've worked there!" your mother says. "John Lewis is the publican."

"I remember him!" cries Zurka.

So they talk about John Lewis, the publican of The White Crown. Your mother seems more relaxed now. You sit listening to them, feeling remorse that a Polish stranger who has chopped people up makes your mother feel more relaxed than her own son.

After a while, Zurka stands up and says he'd better not make a nuisance of himself and he says goodbye to your mother and goes out. You're left, just the two of you together again, except for the screw reading his newspaper. The screw is relieved that Zurka has gone out. The men aren't supposed to get involved with each other's visitors.

"He seems quite nice," your mother says of Zurka.

"Yes, a nice chap," you say.

"A foreigner, isn't he?"

"Polish."

"Has he been here long?"

"Eleven years."

You and your mother have an understanding that hardly anyone is kept in this place very long because, of course, you yourself will only be kept a short while, just until your "nerves" improve. So she doesn't ask why Zurka is here, though she's curious. Anyway, she's clearly glad to have found there are men here as nice as Zurka seems to be.

It's time for her to go.

"My train's at four-fifty," she says.

"Right-o," you say, then you ask about something that's been on your mind for the last few weeks, ever since the night in the television room when you heard the wind in the trees and the clank of the chain on the main gate.

"Er, mum, could you send me a book of poetry?" You feel awkward about using the word "poetry". You don't want her to think you're becoming a poofter or anything like that.

"Poetry?" she says, looking at you.

"Yes, what they call an anthology."

"All right dear, if you want me to."

"Thanks."

You're still feeling awkward about it when you give her a kiss on the cheek and she goes up the corridor with a screw to unlock the door for her. You wave to each other and she goes out the door. You're very glad she came, now, though, and glad that Zurka helped so much. You go round to the window of the television room to see if you can watch her at the main gate. You try to wave to her from there, but she can't see you inside the window with the bars in the way. Then you go back to the dining room and wait while the screw cuts your cake into eight portions to make sure there's nothing concealed in it.

Arthur has a special project and has chosen you for it. He wants a brick-walled compost heap built at the bottom of the vegetable garden, hard against the main wall where the drainage is best.

"Done any bricklaying?" he wants to know.

"None," you say.

"Doesn't matter. You'll pick it up as you go."

So you're given a trowel and a spirit-level and a few tips about mixing mortar and how to make use of string to keep the bricks in line. A load of sand and lime and cement is ordered and, after a week or so, is delivered and dumped near the site.

You're even given a labourer. A bald, bony man of about fifty, named Bob Fleet. Bob Fleet is a homosexual and loves boys' bums. At least, that's what he keeps saying.

"Oh, God, I love a tender young bum!" he says as he mixes a wheelbarrow load of mortar. "Ever fucked a nice little boy?" he asks you.

"Not lately," you say.

The hole for the compost heap has already been dug and you're supposed to wall it on three sides to a height of about four feet. It's good being down in the hole. The earth is damp and smells cold and fresh and there are big pink earthworms sticking out of it. It's also private down there. Sometimes a screw comes to see how you're doing, but mostly they don't bother you. Your head and shoulders just come above the hole and there is long grass and the piles of bricks in front to screen you right off from the ward and from the high spots where the screws sit when they're watching the other men in the garden.

You're still part of the garden gang, but semi-independent because of being out of sight a bit and because Arthur has shown he trusts you with this special work. You're feeling a lot more relaxed now. Arthur can't be thinking of giving you shock or medication, not if he's picked you out for this. He must have talked to Electric Ned too, so that means the doctor must think you're all right. The important thing now is to make a good job of it. After a couple of days you begin to understand about the bricks and how much mortar to use and how to keep testing with the spirit-level and how to adjust your line to the taut string across the top. You get a lot of kidding from the screws and the other men because of being down the hole so much. Jokes about you digging a tunnel under the main wall and stuff like that. Sometimes Arthur comes down from the ward to see how you're doing.

"How's it going?" he asks, checking the line and level with his eye.

"Going like steam," you answer.

"And how's your offsider working?"

"Bob's doing well," you say, but really Bob Fleet is a nuisance. He's getting on your nerves. His talk about fucking boys is getting more and more personal. He wants to know whether you've ever done it yourself and tells you it's wonderful and that you're missing out on something if you don't do it. Then he starts telling you how nice your own bum looks and how he'd love to get into you.

"How'd you like me to make love to you?" he asks.

"I'd rather you didn't thanks."

"You'd like it."

After a while you see that being polite isn't getting you anywhere with Bob Fleet.

"Let me have your sweet bum," he says.

"You can have my sweet fist in your fucking snout if you like!"

"Don't be like that, darling."

"I'm not your darling, you fucking decrepit old mongrel!"

"Yes, you're my darling. I just wish you wouldn't tease me."

"I'll tease you into a mangled blood heap if you're not careful!"

Nothing you say makes any difference to him. You just ignore him and let him talk. Anyway, you can't think of any more insults. At the back of your mind you even feel a little flattered that he's so keen to fuck you. The thought of making love with some beautiful, gentle boy gives you a tiny shiver of excitement, but you push the thought away. Bob Fleet is neither beautiful nor gentle, and you'd rather die than have him touch you. You tell him so.

"I'd rather die than have you touch me!"

He hoots with laughter. "What a pure little virgin! Death before dishonour, eh?"

You realise it did sound funny, like Mary Pickford or someone in the old movies when the villain is tying her on the railway track. You laugh too. After that you begin to like Bob Fleet in a horrible sort of way. His old father was a tram conductor in the 'twenties and 'thirties and Bob talks a lot about his dad's adventures with women passengers. The father liked women, not boys.

"Dad used to feel them up on the tram, specially when it was crowded. Sometimes, if a pretty girl didn't have the fare, he'd offer to let her ride free for a feel of tit. Lots of 'em didn't have the fare during the Depression. Another lurk was to pretend he was gonna hand them over to the cops for avoiding the fare, then offer to let them go for a good feel. Sometimes they were so frightened of the police they'd let him have a proper root. He'd keep them on the tram till he finished his shift, then take them back and root them behind the depot shed. He came unstuck though. A freak coincidence. He tried it on with a passenger who happened to be the wife of the bloke driving the tram. A big fella. He was gonna murder dad. Dad threw his ticket bag in the bloke's face and leapt off the tram and down an alley. He never went back on the trams."

Bob Fleet has a favourite limerick:

"There was a young lady from France
Who fell from the tram in a trance,
The gallant conductor
Leapt down and plucked her
Away from the traffic's advance."
But he always pauses before "plucked her".

Away to the left from where you're working in the hole is the swimming pool and you can see Ray Hoad vacuuming the bottom with a long pole that has a suction nozzle on the end. Being the pool man is the best job of all. It's privileged. The pool man can go down to work whenever he wants during the day and without any screws to watch him. The pool man works the chlorinating equipment too, and if he doesn't do it right he could gas everyone, so you don't get to be pool man unless Arthur and Electric Ned are very sure about you.

Bob Fleet is after Ray Hoad too. He calls Ray his "wife".

"Oh Ray, my wife, let me have you!" he calls out.

"You can root my boot on your birthday!" Ray Hoad yells back.

You've got the brickwork finished. It's been three weeks and it looks good. Arthur is pleased. They start heaping grass and rotten vegetables and other stuff into the hole to let it turn into compost. Then one of the supervisors from Administration comes around and notices how the new brickwork joins the main wall up to about four feet and he's worried that it might provide a foothold for anyone trying to scale the wall and escape. Arthur doesn't think it will, because there's still sixteen feet of sheer wall above.

The supervisor isn't convinced, and says that part of the new brickwork must be knocked down.

***

You've been moved from the corner table in the dining room, away from the messy eaters and the disturbed men. You're now at the best table, with Bill Greene, Ray Hoad, Zurka and a couple more. It's much nicer; you can talk while you're eating, and you can ask for the salt to be passed and someone will pass it. Grumps is there too. He doesn't talk much, except to swear and groan softly under his breath, but it's good having him at your table because he never eats his lunchtime dessert and always lets one of the others have it. You're right across the table from Grumps, so he usually pushes it across to you.

The men are put at different tables according to how well they are, and according to what the screws call their "level of socialisation". Being at this table means that the screws are satisfied with you and you can feel relaxed because hardly anyone at this table ever gets shock or very heavy medication. But if something happens and you get shifted back to one of the other tables, you know you're in trouble.

You're at the table one morning at breakfast time, waiting for the meal to be passed through the servery and brought to you. You notice that there's a tiny bit of dried food on your spoon from the last man who used it. You aren't bothered by it much, but you're trying to scrape the fragment off with your fingernail.

"What are you doing?" comes a friendly voice over your shoulder. It's a big, blond screw called Smiler.

You show him the spoon with the dried fragment on it.

"I was just trying to scrape this stuff off," you say.

He takes the spoon and examines it. "It wasn't washed properly," he says. Then he says in the same friendly voice: "Why don't you go and ask for a clean one?"

Maybe your mind isn't very alert today, or maybe you're too relaxed by being at the best table.

"Right," you say, and you go over to the servery and call to one of the pantry workers. "Hey Freddie, would you give me a clean spoon, please?"

Suddenly there's a dead silence and everyone is watching you. You realise Smiler has set you up like a pigeon. You can hardly believe your own stupidity. Arthur is inside the servery. He takes the spoon and examines it very slowly and carefully, holding it up to light as though it's a holy relic or something. Then he hands the spoon back.

"You're getting very fastidious, aren't you?" Arthur says in a voice that makes your veins run cold.

You take the spoon and go back to your seat and have your meal, though you can hardly eat for worrying about what will happen. You see Smiler grinning. It went so perfectly.

At dinner time you go into the dining room with the other men and you're about to sit at your normal place when Smiler says: "You've been shifted, Tarbutt." He motions you to the corner table, the worst table of all. You sit down and try to look calm. Being at this table means that the shadow of shock and medication is on you. For three days you stay at the corner table, being terribly careful about every look and move and gesture you make.

You tell yourself that you'll be all right. You remember how pleased Arthur seemed with you over the bricklaying and everything, and surely they wouldn't give you shock just because of the spoon. You can't be sure though, so you go about for the three days with a pain in your stomach from worry.

On the fourth day after the spoon, you're going in to the dining room again and another screw motions you back to your old place at the best table and you know then that they'd just been giving you a little lesson. You know they won't be forgetting about the spoon though, not for a long time, and you're going to have to be very careful for a long time.

Barry Clarke has been taken off some of his medication. He's not dribbling and wetting himself any more and can talk almost normally and work a bit in the vegetable garden. He's lost a photo of his wife and baby daughter. He thinks Hartley stole it. Hartley is a famous murderer who killed five men and cut off their balls because he was molested by a sergeant in the army. Hartley knows he'll be in this place until he dies. We're having breakfast and Barry Clarke is looking across at Hartley as if he wants to smash him and is muttering horrible curses. Suddenly Barry Clarke goes berserk. He leaps up and heaves the table over so that all the food and the plates go onto the floor. Then he picks up his chair and hurls it at Hartley's head. Hartley knows straight away what's happening and he runs for the door. It's unlocked. Just as he's about to disappear, the chair catches him on the back of the head. He staggers in mid stride and then is gone.

Five or six screws surround Barry Clarke. He's quiet now but is trembling and his face is white. The screws take him outside, and Arthur takes Hartley into the office to dress the gash in his head.

Barry Clarke isn't punished very much, just given extra medication again. The screws don't worry so much about fights like that because fights between inmates don't really threaten their authority. Not like the dirty spoon. The dirty spoon threatened them.

Ray Hoad was just about to eat his egg when Barry's table banged into him. His egg went on the floor.

"What about my egg!" he kept saying. "I want another egg!" He thinks it's very unfair.

If you do something violent like Barry Clarke they sometimes put you in the "grille", a sort of wire cage, like a monkey cage at the zoo, which is at the end of the verandah. We think maybe they didn't put Barry there because it's already occupied. Skippy's been in the grille for weeks. He has an abnormal brain and whenever they let him out he attacks the first person he sees. Skippy seems very much like the orang-utans you see at the zoo. He sits all crumpled up in the cage, staring out through the wire mesh with red, sunken eyes and flexing his hands and rubbing his lips together slowly. He seems so quiet in the grille that every couple of weeks the screws decide to let him out, but he turns wild and has to be put back. They say Skippy is going to be sent away for an operation on his brain.

You're talking to Zurka about what he did to the people with his butcher's chopper. He doesn't mind talking about it now. He's pretty sure he's to be transferred to the open section and he wants to show that he understands about his crime and why he did it and that it was a dreadful act. The screws say that being able to talk calmly about your crime shows you've gained insight. Of course, you mustn't talk about it too much, or too calmly, or they'll say you're dwelling on it or that you aren't showing a healthy remorse.

"I had this belief that somebody was after me," he says.

"Who?"

"I didn't know exactly. Spies, or something."

"Why were they after you, did you think?"

"Because of my feet."

"Your feet?"

"Yes, I believed that my feet gave off a terrible stink, and that everyone could smell them, and that the spies or whatever they were could follow the smell of my feet."

"Did you wash your feet?"

"Yes, ten times a day, but it made no difference. I still thought they stank in a peculiar way. Different from normal smelly feet. Foul. Horrible."

"Did you ever try to get help?"

"I went to psychiatrists. Tons of them. They just gave me expensive pills that I couldn't afford. In my mind I knew that the thing about the feet was caused by mental illness, but I couldn't snap myself out of it."

"The expensive pills didn't do any good?"

"I couldn't afford them. The psychiatrists would give me a prescription for pills but I didn't have the money to get them all the time. I could hardly afford to pay the psychiatrists' fees."

"But there were free clinics and stuff like that."

"I didn't know about them. I didn't have anyone to advise me, and my English wasn't so good then. I just didn't know anything, except to spend all my money going to private psychiatrists who fobbed me off with pills."

"Weren't there Polish groups that could have helped or advised you?"

"Bah! My own countrymen didn't want to know me. They are bastards! Bastards!"

"And what actually happened, on the train?"

"I started carrying a butcher's chopper to protect myself. That day I was on the train and I thought the spies were getting close. I thought they were coming along the train, through the carriages to get me, maybe throw me off. Then I saw that the other passengers were staring at me in a funny way, as if they knew what was going to happen. I suddenly thought that they were the spies and that they had false faces on. Plastic faces or something to disguise themselves and that underneath the false faces they were really the spies and that they were grinning and laughing, knowing they finally had me cornered. I knew I only had a minute left before they pulled off their faces and killed me."

"So you decided to defend yourself?"

"I pulled out the chopper and went at them. I think I was screaming with terror, but I thought I'd get some of them before they got me. I was trying to chop through their plastic faces."

"It must have been very horrible."

"It was very horrible. The blood and the faces coming open and everyone screaming. I don't know how it ended. I fainted or something, after I'd chopped a few people."

Zurka is obviously very sorry and sad when he's telling about the last bit, about the train. You are quite sure he'd never do anything like that again. You'd bet your bones on it. If it was up to you, you'd let Zurka go to the open section. Yet when he's talking about the psychiatrists who took all his money for pills and fees, or about his Polish countrymen who wouldn't help him, you get a faint cold feeling of worry. There's an edge in his voice that makes you think he's spent the years here remembering the wrong they did him. It's probably nothing. You'd still let him go to the open section if the decision was up to you. Yet you're glad, somehow, that it's someone else's decision.

Everyone is confident for Zurka. While you're sitting with him, Eddie comes up the verandah. He's got a brown parcel.

"Won't be faaarkin long now, Zurka," he says. "The transfer'll be through any day."

Zurka nods and smiles.

"You'll be in faaarkin clover in the faaarkin open section. Puttin' all the faaarkin sheilas up the faaarkin duff."

Zurka smiles again, but shakes his head a little to show he has no intention of doing anything so irresponsible. You understand his position. The screws are watching him all the time now, gauging his mental attitude towards the transfer. If he seems too eager it might look bad. If he doesn't seem eager enough it might look bad.

Eddie remembers the parcel.

"Faaarkin parcel for ya, Len," he says, handing it over.

You start unwrapping it so that Eddie can see the contents. All letters and parcels have to be opened in front of a screw.

"Nobody sends me any faaarkin parcels," he's grumbling. "You blokes are faaarkinwell spoiled rotten. If I was in control you'd all be on faaarkin bread 'n faaarkin water with chains on ya faaarkin legs."

Your heart gives a little leap when you unwrap the last of the paper. It's a book, *Best English Poems: Chaucer to the Present Day*.

There's a spot at the far end of the verandah where you like to sit and be alone sometimes. Of course you can't really be alone, because of the other men pacing up and down near you, or lying along the benches beside you, or because the toilets are just next to your spot and there are always men there talking and smoking while they're on the lavatory. The toilets have little low half doors on the front and you can always see somebody's head and shoulders above the top and their feet at the bottom with trousers crumpled around them. A couple of screws are always on watch on the verandah so that you're under observation. But you can sit there in your spot and look out at the lake through the wire and not talk to anyone and pretend that you're almost alone. You have to be careful not to overdo it, that's all. If the screws see you sitting quiet and staring too often, they'll think you're too withdrawn and might report it to the doctor. So you space out your alone periods. You make sure the screws see you playing billiards or cards, or see you talking and laughing with other men. When you've let them see you doing those things for a while you know it's probably safe to go to your spot and try to be alone for maybe an hour. If you do it for more than an hour you're taking a risk.

Your new book of poems has a dark green cover and gold coloured lettering down the spine. You sit in your spot on the verandah and run your hands over the cover and the lettering and then flick the pages over so that you see a fast blur of print. The pages are very white and fresh and smell nice. You haven't started to read it yet. You want to get used to the lovely feel of the book first. It's only a cheap book, because your mother hasn't got much money, but it's got a beautiful feel. There's another reason you haven't started to read it yet. You feel a little afraid to start, in case you find that poetry isn't what you expected.

Your eye falls on a line of a poem near the back of the book:

"The naked earth is warm with spring."

The poem is called "Into Battle" and that first line gives you a faint prickle of excitement.

"The naked earth is warm with spring
And with green grass and bursting trees
Leans to the sun's gaze glorying,
And quivers in the sunny breeze;"

Oh, it's lovely. The hairs on the back of your neck are prickling right up.

"And life is colour and warmth and light,
And a striving evermore for these;
And he is dead who will not fight;
And who dies fighting has increase."

It's giving you that same strong feeling you got from the *Bible* words about going through the valley of the shadow of death.

"The fighting man shall from the sun
Take warmth, and life from the glowing earth;
Speed with the light-foot winds to run,
And with the trees to newer birth;
And find, when fighting shall be done,
Great rest and fullness after dearth."

A whole new world is flooding into you. A whole new way of thinking about birds and sunlight and the sun's gaze glorying. And then the poem goes on to the end about:

"Through joy and blindness he shall know,

Not caring much to know, that still
Nor lead nor steel shall touch him, so
That it not be the Destined Will."
And then the deep music, like an organ, of the finish:
"The thundering line of battle stands,
And in the air death moans and sings,
But Day shall clasp him with strong hands,
And Night shall fold him in soft wings."
You look round when the screw taps you on the shoulder and
see that the verandah is empty. Everyone's gone in for breakfast.
The screw looks oddly at you, but for once you don't care
whether he reports you for acting strangely. Life is wonderful
and you can face anything!

4

You're not the new man any more. Two others have come since you got here. One of them is Dick Steele, a short, tough "crim" who is doing six years for trying to blast another "crim" with gelignite. He's got a slow, cold way of looking at you sometimes, as though he's full of a deep rage and is thinking of the best way to cripple you. But some of the time Dick Steele is very entertaining and tells vivid little stories of the underworld:

"...Jigger Mottram done this big bust, see, and got nine fur coats. Lovely stuff. He takes 'em to Quinn, who's his usual fence, and Quinn says he'll give him eight 'undred for 'em. Jigger won't cop it. He reckons they're worth two thousand. So they start arguin' and Quinn tells Jigger ter piss orf or he'll hand 'im up ter the jacks, see. Doesn't say it straight out, just sorta hints about it. Well, Jigger won't wear a nark, so he decides to knock Quinn orf, see, and goes back the next night full o' grog and walks in the door and lets both barrels go at Quinn. Quinn rolls down behind the sofa and comes up with a pistol and lets go at Jigger while he's reloadin', see ..."

Dick Steele gathers a little circle of hangers-on around him. Dave Lamming is one of them. Dave has recovered from the shock treatment now but is very timid and nervous and spends a lot of time cleaning windows. He's frightened of Dick Steele and the fear makes him do whatever he's told. Dick Steele seems to get his only pleasure from a series of deadly feuds with certain other men. He hates Mario in particular and does everything possible to niggle the Sicilian, then drifts away leaving Dave to face the onslaught. But Dick Steele isn't a coward. Already he's had several fights with men bigger than himself and has won them. Only once have you felt the full force of his hatred. Dick is rostered to watch television on the same night as you. Last week you got up and changed the channel, unaware that Dick was engrossed in the programme. He didn't protest, but just started quietly cursing you with terrible oaths. You quickly changed the channel back. Dick Steele seems able to get any kind of illicit goods. When no screws are looking, he'll pull out a bottle of wine and pass it around, insisting that everyone take a swig. This is probably meant to implicate us all, so that nobody will rat on him. He is said to have a knife, and we believe it.

The other new man is Sam Lister, a good looking and intelligent man of about thirty. He's here for one unsuccessful attempt at arson, the only crime he's ever committed. He was disturbed in his mind when he did it, but is quite normal now. Soon after he came here you got a foolish idea that he had something against you. The idea preyed on you for a long time, until one day you went up to him, trembling and shaky-voiced, and offered to settle it with fists. Sam was very understanding and sat and talked quietly to you, convincing you that you'd been under a misapprehension. Now you have interesting talks with him about the meaning of life and things like that. Sam Lister is the only one you can talk to about your interest in poetry. Sam talks a lot about something called TA, a method of understanding your own inner feelings and how to keep them in balance. He says that every person really has three personalities inside them. The Child, the Adult and the Parent, and that when we feel helpless and afraid it's because we are acting out the Child part of ourselves, the part that we subconsciously remember from the time when we really were small and vulnerable. And when we feel stern and intolerant and disapproving of ourselves it's because we are acting the Parent role. The best thing, Sam says, is try to let the Adult part be in control, the part that's sensible and insightful. The Adult part is in the middle and balances the unhappy extremes of the other two. Sam talks a lot about Inner Balance, which he says is the secret of life.

"Tell me about your life," Sam says to you. You are sitting with him on the verandah in the bright morning sun, feeling the cramp of the cell and the long night being warmed out of you.

So you start telling him about everything in your past and how and why you did the thing that you got the Life Sentence for. After a while, the nervousness vanishes and you find you enjoy telling Sam about yourself. He's such a good listener. Soon you and Sam are spending most of your free time together and your life story is drawing out longer and longer, like a serial. Every so often, though, you get a bit afraid again that it's too uninteresting to bother with.

"I told you it would bore you," you say.

"Don't start that again."

"Sorry."

Whenever we have free time together and Sam wants to hear more of your life story, he'll say, "Back to the couch!"

"The couch" is our joke, as though Sam is my psychiatrist or something. Now we are lying on the grass near the pool. The other men are splashing and yelling, but we'd rather talk. We're lying full length with our faces near each other. Sam is chewing a stem of grass. It's lovely, lying there in the sun with Sam, talking about things which you want to try to understand about your life, but which would be too painful to even think about if you were just by yourself. Even the embarrassing things, like never having had a girlfriend. Even those things are easy to talk to Sam about. The swimming time is over and the screws are ready to take us back into the ward.

"Is there hope for me, doctor?" you say to Sam.

"I'm not sure yet. I'll have to hear more. I may be able to save you from the asylum."

"Oh good!"

"Twenty guineas please."

You reach for an imaginary wallet.

"Pay my secretary."

"Your secretary?"

"Yes, Miss Fifi LaRue. An interesting case of nymphomania."

"Are you curing her?"

"Are you mad?"

A children's charity has sent bits of broken toys to be repaired and Arthur has made a workshop in an old shed near the sports field, just behind the trees you like so much. Each day seven men and two screws go across to paint tricycles, patch dolls' dresses, put stuffing into teddy bears and reassemble tiny tea sets.

The first day we went to clean up the shed. It hadn't been used for years and it had cobwebs and dust and piles of rubbish. In a corner were boxes of old files, dating back to the nineteen-thirties. We read some of them when the screws weren't watching. There were ward reports on inmates of the time and told how so-and-so was eating shit and someone else had cut his own throat. It must have been very bad in those days before effective medication, when men just stayed raging mad and violent for years, trussed in straightjackets and locked in cells all day and night. It makes you wonder about medication nowadays, whether it's better to be made into a zombie, like now, or be left to shriek and scream and eat shit like in the old days. But you can't believe the old files totally. They were written by screws and screws always make the inmates sound very bad. It makes the screws feel like tough men. Lion tamers or something. A lot of screws are touchy about being male nurses. Sometimes they get picked on in the pub when they're off duty, because of being male nurses. So they like to pretend they're lion tamers, holding beasts away from the women and children. And when they've made the inmates seem very dangerous, they pretend to shrug off the danger, to show what cool nerves of steel they have. They get danger money for working here, and if they didn't make the inmates seem very dangerous they might not get the danger money. Nobody gets danger money for taming pussy cats. Still, the old files make you think that maybe it was pretty bad here in the old days and that maybe the screws who wrote those files weren't exaggerating much.

The toy repairing is nice work, once you get over the silly feeling.

"Do we get paid for this?" Ray Hoad wants to know.

"Your reward will be the rosy cheeks of smiling little tots," says Bill Greene.

"Frig the tots!" answers the Merry Dwarf.

Hartley, the famous murderer, is fitting a red piece on a fire engine. The screws don't usually like Hartley to leave the verandah area, but he's been allowed to join the Merry Band. Ray Hoad and Bill Greene say he murders dolls when nobody's looking.

After a few weeks a man from the children's charity comes to tell us how much our work is appreciated. He's a short, tubby man. He appears in the doorway with Arthur. The charity man steps in cautiously as if he's afraid someone will grab his throat. He stays close to Arthur.

"Chaps," Arthur says, "this is Mr Fleming from the charity."

We all stare at Mr Fleming. He's trying to look all jolly, like a man representing thousands of happy children. He obviously has a little speech ready, but he can't seem to get it out. It's probably just dawned on him that he's actually inside this place and face to face with seven Criminally Insane men who are staring intently at him and maybe aching to rip his gullet.

His big grin keeps slipping off and he has to push it back up his chin.

"Um, er, we just wanted to let you people know how grateful we are..." He trails off, as though suddenly wondering whether we understand normal English. He's glancing uneasily around, perhaps thinking how there are only three screws here against seven of us.

"You're doing wonderful work here, er, um, chaps." He isn't too sure about calling us "chaps". Calling us "chaps" might offend us. But Arthur had called us "chaps" so he thinks it must be all right. If Arthur had called us "Your Excellencies", Mr Fleming would call us that too.

"Er, well, that's really about all I wanted to say," says Mr Fleming. He looks at Arthur, wondering whether to go now.

"Did you have something to give the chaps?" prompts Arthur gently, indicating something Mr Fleming has in his hand.

"Oh yes!" Mr Fleming remembers. He has a little framed certificate. "Er, we at the charity wish to present you chaps with a token of our appreciation." He goes to hold out the framed certificate to one of us, but isn't sure who to offer it to. He takes a step toward Hartley but falters and steps back. Nobody moves. It's a terrible moment for Mr Fleming. He'd probably imagined it differently. He'd probably imagined a jolly visit, with lots of back-slapping and himself making a confident little speech and someone stepping forward to shake his hand and then more back-slapping and applause. Now he's standing here with his framed certificate held out in the empty air while seven silent madmen stare at him. The screws are enjoying it too.

"Thanks very much," you say to him.

One of us has spoken! He's so relieved, he goes to put out his hand to shake yours, but loses his nerve and lets it drop.

"We're glad to help the poor kiddies," says Ray Hoad.

"And the tiny tots," says Bill Greene.

"The dear little ones."

"The darlings."

Mr Fleming is beaming now and hopping about shaking hands with all of us, except Hartley. Hartley is wearing a grin like Dracula and Mr Fleming sort of bypasses his handshake, as though by an oversight. Ray Hoad and Bill Greene want to go on some more about the Darling Tots and the Wee Kiddies, but Arthur has given them a warning look. They've had their fun.

"Well, I suppose I should be going now," says Mr Fleming, as if going is the last thing he wants to do but has a schedule to keep. He goes out with Arthur, smiling and waving back at us.

"Bye bye," calls Ray Hoad. "Give our love to the Wee Ones."

"And the Totties."

"And the Snotties."

"And the Potties."

But Mr Fleming has gone, back to tell his battleaxes what a decent bunch of chaps we are.

You're digging over a vegetable bed one morning and Arthur strolls down.

"What do you think of books?" he asks.

"How do you mean?"

"Think our fellows need them?"

"Well, reading is a good pastime."

The hospital is supposed to have a library, but it's over in the open section and we don't have access to it. All we have here are a few old books piled up on a shelf at the end of the verandah where the cards and dominoes and chess set are kept. The books are falling to pieces because the rain has been blowing in under the verandah on them for years. They aren't very interesting anyway, mainly detective stories, and you never see anyone reading them. You wonder why Arthur is suddenly concerned with books.

"I've had an approach from the librarian," he says. "She's new on the job and pretty keen. She wants our chaps to have access to her stuff."

"Good idea," you say.

"Someone will have to handle it from this end. On a weekly basis," he says. "Are you interested?"

"I'll have a go," you say.

"Good. The librarian is coming over this morning to talk to you about it." This is an interesting turn. Arthur has been a bit distant with you ever since the dirty spoon, and now he's chosen you for this. You think your stocks must be rising again. An hour later a screw calls you up from the garden and you go into the office. Arthur is there with a young woman of about twenty-two. She is slim and nice looking, with long brown hair. Arthur introduces you. Her name's Marian.

"Your Charge tells me you'd like to help me extend the library service into this ward," she says. Her voice is very assured and educated, like a school mistress.

"Yes."

"Excellent," she says. She gives you a big smile. "I gather you read a lot yourself?"

"Oh, a good deal," you say. It seems the right answer.

Marian is wearing a miniskirt and it is right up near her thighs. Her legs are long and very beautiful. You try to keep looking her right in the eyes because if you don't concentrate on her eyes, you know your glance will keep going down to her legs and then she'll know you're not the nice bookworm she thinks you are.

"Your Charge tells me you like poetry," she says.

"Er, yes," you say.

"Do you write any yourself?"

"Oh, a little bit," you say. You feel awkward about that. You'd rather not tell anyone about the poems you've been trying

57

to write. You'd prefer to keep all that quiet and safe inside yourself, but Marian obviously wants to hear you say that you write poetry and you want very much to please Marian. You want her to give you another big smile that makes your insides quiver. She does.

You can see a few men out on the verandah looking in through the glass partition at Marian. They're envying you being right in the office with this girl and so close to her beautiful legs.

"Who are your favourite authors?" she asks.

"Oh, I suppose Julian Grenfell's my favourite."

"Who?"

"Julian Grenfell."

"I don't know him," she says. "What did he write?"

You feel slightly shocked. Surely she knows the author of the wonderful "Into Battle"? You start to think that maybe you don't like Marian as much as you thought.

"He was a war poet, in the trenches."

"Oh, like Wilfred Owen?"

"That's right!" you say, warming to her again. "Do you like Wilfred Owen?"

"Oh yes, his verse is lovely," she says.

You're liking Marian a lot now. Wilfred Owen is in your book, on the next page from Julian Grenfell, and on the nearby pages are other war poets like Isaac Rosenberg and Siegfried Sassoon.

"Do you know Owen's poem 'Futility'?" you ask.

"Um, I'm not sure," she says. "How does it go?"

You know exactly how it goes because it's all you've been thinking of for days. You recite the first lines to Marian:

> *"Move him into the sun.*
> *Gently its touch awoke him once,*
> *At home, dreaming of fields unsown.*
> *Always it woke him, even in France,*
> *Until this morning and this snow.*
> *If anything might rouse him now*
> *The kind old sun will know."*

While you're saying the words, the beauty of them strikes you all over again, so that you speak them very clearly and feelingly and you even start to make a little gesture with your hand, like an actor or something. Then you see that Marian is smiling a lovely smile at you, and Arthur is looking at you closely and smiling a little too. You suddenly feel embarrassed. It's incredible. You've been spouting poetry right here in the office, in front of people.

"That's beautiful," Marian says.

"Oh, it's not bad," you say, wondering if she thinks you're a fool.

"Well, about the books," she says, suddenly getting businesslike. "Each week you'll go around to all the men here and take a list of what sort of books each man wants, then your Charge will send the list over to me and I'll send a boxful of selected titles back over on the food truck, and you'll distribute them to the men and gather them up again the following week to be exchanged for a new lot. All right?"

"Fine."

"Of course, I can't guarantee that each borrower will get exactly what he asks for, but I'll make the selection as close to each one's preference as I can. I'm afraid, in your own case, I don't have much in the way of poetry."

"Never mind," you say, "anything will do." You don't really want to read any other poetry books, it would be like betraying your own lovely green book with the gold coloured lettering.

"It's settled then," Marian says. She gives you another big smile. You realise the talk is over, so you stand up to go and Marian puts out her hand and you shake with her. Her hand feels nice in yours, soft and firm. As you go out of the office you hear Marian say to Arthur: "He seems a nice boy."

You don't hear Arthur's reply.

The other men all want to hear about Marian and what it was like being so close to her.

"Did you get a feel of her?" Bill Greene wants to know.

"Of course not. We were talking about literature."

"Literature be fucked!" says Ray Hoad.

"We heard you was rootin' her on the floor," says Bill.

"Chock-a-block up her," says Ray.

"With Arthur ticklin' ya balls with a feather," says Bill.

You just grin and let them talk.

"I'd like to get into her."

"I'd fuck her arse off!"

"She'd love it!"

"Course she would."

"Did yer see the miniskirt?"

"Yeah, she's a fuckin' prickteaser!"

"Flashin' her fanny!"

"She likes Len."

"Because he's got a cock like a horse."

"They were talkin' about literature."

"On the floor."

"She was talkin' and Len was fuckin'."

Tuesday is the day for you to go around to all the men and make a list of books they want. Most of them aren't very interested. You approach Hartley, the famous murderer.

"How many books can I order?" he asks.

"Four or five," you say.

"I want five books about murder," he says.

"What for? Homework?" says Ray Hoad, who's nearby.

So you write it down. "Hartley. Five books on murder."

"Er, don't you think it might look a bit odd?" you ask him.

"Why?" he asks.

"Well, just saying 'about murder' like that. If the screws see the list, they might think you're dwelling on the subject."

"I am," he says quietly.

"Oh," you say and quickly move on to the next man. Later you change the "about murder" to "about crime".

Hartley will never get out. He doesn't care. At least, he says he doesn't. He says he'll die happy, knowing that he's killed several people. When his first batch of books comes he's very pleased because one of them is about famous Australian murderers and he has a whole chapter in it, with photographs of himself handcuffed between policemen and pictures of the victims' bodies and the places where the killings happened. Ray Hoad says the book is Hartley's family album.

Hartley is very musical. He used to be allowed to play an old dusty piano locked away in one of the storerooms. He played very well, Mozart and stuff like that, but the screws stopped him playing after a few months because of security. They always talk about "security" whenever they want to stop anyone doing anything. Then Hartley got a violin sent to him and was allowed to play it for a couple of weeks until someone realised he might use the strings to strangle people, so they took the violin away. You think maybe they were right about the violin, but the piano seemed harmless.

"Who ever heard of anyone being strangled with a piano?" Bill Greene says.

"He murdered Mozart with it, didn't he?" suggests Ray Hoad.

Dick Steele is making everyone edgy. His feuds with other men have got very savage and there's an undercurrent of violence. Mario has already attacked Dick with a billiard cue, really trying to smash Dick's head. Dick got away unhurt, but he's still goading Mario. It's bad in the television room, when you're locked up with him for three and a half hours and he sits up at the back and weaves a web of hatred over the room. If one of his enemies is there he'll niggle and goad all night in lots of little ways. He always brings his bottle of wine out and makes everyone share it, and you dare not refuse. He keeps pressing you as though he's just being very friendly, but if you keep refusing he makes you one of his enemies. Even Ray Hoad doesn't want to get on the bad side of him. You know Dick is mad, in an even worse way than Hartley, but he doesn't show it, especially when screws are about. Dick is close to several of the screws and you have a feeling there's some sort of arrangement between them, maybe for getting the wine. Dick has a kind of power which you feel, but can't quite explain. You never talk ill of Dick with anyone, because he might overhear, or because you're afraid the person you talk to might report your comments to Dick. He makes you feel he has ears everywhere, like the secret police or something.

It's making you very tense. You're sure something bad will happen in the ward sooner or later. Maybe a stabbing.

You're in the billiard room. Dick is lolling in a chair. He wants a cushion from across the room.

"Get me a cushion, Len," he says.

You know this is a tricky moment, a sort of test for you. If you go and get the cushion you'll be showing that you're weak and afraid of him, like Dave Lamming, and he'll have you fetching and carrying for him all the time. If you refuse, he'll start marking you down on his enemy list.

You look over at him, as though you hadn't heard properly.

"Pardon?" you say, making your voice flat.

"Get me that cushion, will you?"

You look across at the cushion and then back at Dick as though you don't quite understand. Dick knows that you do understand.

"You want a cushion?"

"Yeah."

You sit quite still. Dick knows that you're going to be difficult.

"I've got a crook back, mate," he says. "I need the cushion for support."

He said that so you can obey him without seeming to lose face. As though you're just helping a bloke with a crook back. He also said it so he'll have a bigger grievance if you defy him, a bigger reason to make you an enemy. You are such a mongrel you wouldn't even do a sick man a tiny favour.

You're at the moment of truth now, and must either obey or defy him. Either way, your life is going to be made miserable from this moment on. You'll be his stooge or his enemy. His face is very grim. You may already have hesitated too long. Just then Bill Greene, who is on the other side of the room, picks up the cushion and throws it as though playfully at Dick's head. The crisis is over. You're not sure whether Bill Greene understood what was happening and deliberately helped you, but you feel grateful anyway.

Sometimes, when Arthur comes down to the vegetable garden and you're talking to him a little away from the other men and screws, you almost tell him of the pressure building up in the ward because of Dick. It's the only time you'd dare, down in the open with just the two of you and no other ears to hear. It would be a very serious thing to do. It would make you a nark, a phizzgig, the lowest form of life. Also, if it got back to Dick that you'd ratted on him, he'd never rest till he'd paid you off. You try to imagine what it feels like to have a knife in your stomach. So you don't say anything to Arthur.

The climax comes in a strange way. One morning Dick comes into the dining room with the others and he's got a long gash down his face. It's raw and bleeding. Arthur wants to know what happened. Dick won't say.

"They got me, that's all," he mutters.

"Who got you?" Arthur wants to know.

"I'm not sayin'."

So Dick is taken into the office. A senior supervisor is called from the other part of the hospital. The supervisor takes a dim view of it, examining Dick's wound and then coming into the dining room to stare at all of us, as if trying to pick the vicious assailant. We see screws moving around the ward. They're searching for the weapon that wounded Dick. The atmosphere is very tight and bad, the screws all with hard faces that they get when there's trouble like this. There's a rumour going among the men that Dick inflicted the wound on himself.

"You know that big nail in the wall on the verandah? He shoved his own face onto it."

"Why?"

"Because he's fuckin' mad!"

"He's trying to frame someone."

"He hates himself!"

"He'll have ter join the queue!"

We don't see Dick any more. We learn he's been locked up in a far cell. Then we hear he's making confessions. About the wine, for instance. Screws open the ceiling of the shower room and find a cache of wine there. Then screws are sent to search behind one of the toilet cisterns and find a long knife, Dick's own. Then it's said that Dick has confessed to having buried a revolver somewhere in the vegetable gardens. By the afternoon two dozen screws have come from outside with long sharp iron rods and are moving methodically across the vegetable gardens, poking the rods down every few inches, hoping to strike the metal of the buried gun. For two days they poke the earth. The gardening work is stopped and all the men kept locked on the verandah under close watch. The screws can't find any gun.

"A bloke feels like a faaarkin idiot," Eddie complains. "Pokin' the faaarkin ground all day."

Once they thought they'd found something. The screws all hurried to the spot and dug a huge hole to unearth something solid that a rod had struck, but it was only a rock. Then a man from the army comes with a mine detector and goes slowly over the whole surface again, but can't find any buried metal. The screws decide there isn't any gun.

After a couple more days, Dick is sent away to the gaol. We all breathe easier, as though we've been freed from a tyrant. For a long time there are jokes about growing guns in the garden.

It's winter. There are a lot of wet days and we don't go to work in the garden when it's raining. When we can't go down to work we have billiard and snooker tournaments, with all the men and some screws gathered all day long in the billiard room. It's snug in there. It has a big old wood-burning heater and some of the men sit around it like Alaskans, yarning and joking, while others are playing or watching the billiards. You can see the rain on the windows and hear the wind and rain whooshing along the verandah or making a low moaning sound in the barbed wire. Sometimes if you want to go out on to the verandah you can hardly push the door open because the wind is blowing so strongly against it, and when you step out you get soaked in a few seconds. But it's good to stand out in the cold and wet for a while on the deserted verandah, looking out across the wall at the mist covering the lake. The best thing about it is that it's so good for thinking about poetry out there, with nobody near, and your mind alert from the cold. The sound of the barbed wire and the wildness of rain makes you think of Flanders, and you can recite some of Wilfred Owen's or Siegfried Sassoon's poems to yourself and they seem even more real and true than ever, as though the trenches were just the other side of the mist. You can feel the sorrow and tragedy running down inside your mind like the rain down the window, then a kind of sombre, piercing happiness at the way the poetry turns all that suffering against itself and rises above it. But you don't stay out there too long or the screws might think you're acting oddly. They wouldn't understand why anyone would enjoy being out in the rain and cold. You're careful not to let your lips move too much either, when you're reciting to yourself. You've already had trouble about them seeing your lips move.

You were in the garden, digging, and during your breathers you were reciting some verses softly to yourself. A screw reported you to Arthur and you were called to the office.

"How d'you feel within yourself, Len?" he wanted to know.

"Good," you said, suddenly feeling very nervous. You know that when a screw asks you how you're feeling within yourself it means they suspect you're disturbed.

"No worries?"

"None in particular. Why?"

"Oh, we just wondered."

They're always like that. They don't come straight out and ask "Why were you talking to yourself?" They just beat around it and make you very nervous, so that unless you're careful, the nervousness will make you say something silly that will confirm their idea that you're disturbed. Anyway, they figure that if you're mentally ill you won't know you're mentally ill and so there's no point asking you about it straight out.

So you just waited while Arthur looked at you thoughtfully and hoped he'd say something to give you a clue.

"We noticed how you seemed a bit agitated this morning, while you were digging."

"Oh," you said, suddenly understanding. "I was just reciting some verse to myself."

"I see," said Arthur. He was still looking closely at you. You could tell he was a little reassured. You didn't deny talking to yourself.

"It's hard to recite verse to yourself without moving your lips," you explained.

"Mmmm, I can see it would be," he agreed. He was probably wondering whether reciting verse to yourself is abnormal or not. "Well then," he said, "we'll say no more about it, eh?"

You went out of the office, still very uneasy, but feeling you'd probably satisfied Arthur.

"What did Arthur want you for?" asked Zurka.

"To ask 'The Question'."

"Did you tell him?" Zurka grinned.

"Sort of," you grinned back.

Everyone knows "The Question": "How do you feel within yourself?", and the answer: "Through the most convenient orifice."

Since then you've trained yourself to recite with a minimum of lip movement, like a ventriloquist.

We're playing soccer at weekends, if the weather isn't too bad. This is a strong soccer district and many of the screws are good players and take part in our games. This is a golden opportunity for Ray Hoad to push and shove screws around. Sometimes, though, it backfires and the screws push and shove us.

Ray has just been deprived of a free kick by the screw referee. Ray thinks it's unfair. He recaptures the ball and is fouled and takes another free kick. The screw referee is standing two yards from the ball as Ray runs up to boot it. The ball seems to fly sideways from his toe and there's a whacking thud and the screw referee collapses gasping and cursing.

"Ohhhh, you cunt!" the screw croaks. "That was bloody deliberate!"

"It was an accident!" protests Ray with a huge grin.

The other screws gather around their winded mate. They discuss whether Ray should be punished. It's up to the fallen screw. He decides to let it pass. For the rest of the game Ray is followed by a thundering trio of screw players, kicking him, shouldering him, hemming him against the wall, tripping him. Ray doesn't care—he's had his satisfaction. Once you get into a melee and are kicked in the calf of the leg by a screw who meant the kick for Ray. You limp to the sideline and nurse your agony.

There aren't enough young and active men to make up two proper teams. The play is really between the four or five enthusiastic men of each side, with the other men set around the field as stationary obstacles. Some screws who belong to the local soccer club decide we need encouragement and arrange for the local under-sixteens to come and play us. This is a great event for us. For weeks we plan tactics, and train and formulate our team.

On a fine Sunday the under-sixteens arrive in a bus and are let in through the gate. They have some mothers and friends with them. The mothers and friends set themselves at the sideline in folding chairs and with thermos flasks of tea and picnic baskets. The under-sixteens strip down to their playing gear and start limbering up. They look very fit and fast. Then our side trots out. We're in new red shirts and white shorts and proper boots that Arthur requisitioned for us. Arthur has given us a little talk about how important this game will be for establishing a precedent. If it goes well, it could lead to regular sporting contacts with outside teams. He says he had to do a lot of string pulling to get this match agreed to by the Administration. He also says some things about this being wonderful for our resocialisation and rehabilitation, but we don't listen to that part much.

While both sides are limbering up, you and Ray Hoad and Bill Greene are talking with a few of the under-sixteens. They're clean-cut boys and have been told about us.

"Is it true you're all murderers?" one asks.

"Yep, it's true all right," says Ray Hoad.

The boys look at us with big eyes. Ray is giving them some friendly tips.

"See that bloke over there," he says, pointing to our centre-half. "Don't let 'im get his hands anywhere near yer throat."

The boys exchange looks.

"And that other fella," says Ray, indicating our goalie, "don't provoke him."

"They call him 'The Wild Man'," says Bill Greene.

"He looks all right," says one of the boys.

"Don't be fooled," says Ray Hoad. "He goes berserk if you annoy him."

The whistle goes and we take our positions. Then the game is under way. The boys are passing, dribbling, feinting, dashing around us, leaving us flat footed. Only Ray Hoad and one or two others are keeping us afloat. The boys soon have two goals.

At half-time we all suck oranges. Ray is whispering to the boys' centre-forward that our goalie is getting a mad look in his eye and might easily murder the next kid who irritates him.

The second half is like the first. The boys are too fit and fast. They score another goal. Then we make a burst. Bill Greene is making a big run downfield with the ball, towards the boys' goal. He's in the open with only the boy goalie to stop him. Ray Hoad is doing a sort of shrieking hiss at the boy, so the spectators won't hear:

"Watch out! He's a killer! Get out of his way! He'll throttle you!"

The boy is rattled. He believes Ray. His face is terrified, but he won't desert his post even if he has to die. He deflects Bill Greene's shot. A moment later it's all over and everyone's shaking hands and saying the game was a great success.

"We've made the little bastards heroes," says Ray Hoad after the boys have gone. "For years they'll be tellin' how they beat the cut-throats!"

"Yeah, and gettin' into their girlfriends' pants on the strength of it."

5

Zurka has been very patient, waiting through the months until his transfer to the open section is only supposed to be a week or so away, and everyone joking about what he'll do when he gets amongst the women over there. Zurka's great interest is statistics. He can tell you the figures for German coal production or Mexican sugar crops or how many rivets in any famous bridge, stuff like that. All the years he's been here he's been reading up on statistics to keep his mind active and because he likes statistics better than anything. Now he isn't able to think about them at all, because of the uncertainty of his transfer. It's wearing his nerves down, especially since the screws are watching him so hard, and even the screws are getting embarrassed about the delay.

Today it has finally come through.

"Pack your bag, mate!" Arthur calls out to him down the verandah. "We've just had word. You're to be transferred before lunch!"

Arthur is grinning and so are the other screws and all the men. Zurka's grinning most of all. He's getting his few things together into the dirty old bag that he came here with. The bag's been in the storeroom for eleven years. Everyone's slapping Zurka on the back, telling him what a lucky bastard he is and how he'll get among the women. The screws are giving him friendly advice:

"Take it easy the first few months."

"Keep your nose clean and your ear to the ground."

"Watch how the wind's blowin'."

"You'll get on fine."

"You'll be in clover."

"We're all pullin' for ya."

Zurka can't take everything in properly, except that the screws are being very nice and want him to make a go of it. After an hour or so the excitement has calmed a little and Zurka is sitting quietly, talking to various men who want to have a last few words with him. You can see from his face that his feelings are all mixed up. He's been dreaming so long about this moment, that now it's here he doesn't know whether to laugh or cry. He's remembering his eleven years and how these men he's lived with are like his brothers, even the worst of them, even the ones he's never liked. He's feeling an odd kind of shame and embarrassment about leaving them. Already it's different between him and them, as if he's won the lottery and is going away from the old friends he was poor with. The other men feel it too, but try not to show anything except how glad they are for Zurka's sake.

It's almost lunchtime and the car will be here for him soon. Zurka's got his bag ready near the office and is shaking hands with someone. A screw comes out of the office and tells Zurka that Arthur wants a word with him. Zurka goes in. You're watching through the glass partition and can see Arthur and some other screws inside the office. They have very serious faces. Arthur has a piece of paper that looks like a telegram. Arthur is saying something to Zurka and Zurka is staring at him, then he suddenly slumps down in a chair like a man who's been hit. Then Zurka seems to be arguing and waving his hands, then he's slumping in the chair again and holding his head in his hands. Arthur is bending over him with a hand on his shoulder, talking to him while the other screws stand back with their serious faces. One of the screws comes out and you ask him what's happened.

"The transfer's been forbidden!" he snaps. He's angry.

"Forbidden? How? Why?"

"A telegram just came from Head Office, maybe from the Minister himself, saying Zurka's not to be moved out of maximum security under any circumstances. Christ, what a fuck-up!"

"But why?" you ask.

"Don't ask me. All I know is there's been a bloody awful fuck-up!" You sit down on the verandah and think what this might mean for Zurka. A fuck-up like this is very bad, and the higher the fuck-up the worse it is. This one came from Head Office, maybe from the Minister himself. A fuck-up that high can kill you. Now it will be on Zurka's file that his transfer was stopped by Head Office or the Minister, and if anyone ever thinks about a transfer again, maybe after another eleven years, they'll remember how it was stopped from so high this time. They won't care why it was stopped. Maybe nobody knows why it was stopped. They'll just recall that it was stopped from so high and that there must have been a reason for it. The fact that nobody knows the exact reason will make it worse.

The really bad part is that Zurka will be able to think it through just like you're doing. He has a statistical mind that can work things out. It would be better for Zurka if he was stupid.

Zurka stays in the office for a couple of hours, sitting in the chair, while Arthur and Electric Ned talk to him. Then he comes out and goes down the verandah. Nobody speaks to him. There's nothing anyone can say, but they try to show how sorry they are by being quiet and not looking at him too much. He wants to go into his cell for a while. The packed bag is still outside the office. A screw unpacks it and puts it back in the storeroom where it had been for eleven years.

At afternoon tea time they bring the urn out on the verandah. The day is dark and windy now. Arthur asks you to take a cup of tea down to Zurka in the cell. You pour a cup out and select three nice biscuits from the tin. Scotch Fingers. You go down the verandah, into the corridor where the cells are.

You can see he's dead. He's hanging very still by a strip of blanket tied to the top of the window. His tongue and eyes are bulging out. Nobody looks like that unless they're dead.

We're coming in from the vegetable gardens before lunch, all dusty and hot from the work, being counted through the verandah gate in the usual way. The screw who's counting finds one short. He doesn't seem worried at first, thinking he's just miscounted. He counts heads again, carefully, and his expression gets very grim. Other screws go around the ward, identifying each man individually. Ray Hoad is missing. Screws run down to check the pool area. They come back and tell Arthur that the long metal pole of the pool's vacuum cleaner is lying bent and buckled beside the main wall. Arthur quickly orders a bunch of screws to run outside the compound and around through the scrub to the spot on the other side of the wall from the pool. These screws come back to say that the grass there is flattened where Ray Hoad must have jumped down. There's no sign of him now, just thousands of acres of bush and scrub stretching away around the lake and back inland.

Arthur is in the office making phone calls. Some of the screws are pulling their ties off and rolling their shirt sleeves up, getting ready to go searching. There are sounds of cars and trucks arriving outside the main gate, and a lot of voices. The search parties are being organised. Everybody's trying to think what Ray Hoad's strategy will be.

"He'll head for the highway and try to hitch a ride."

"Nah, he won't have time. There'll be road blocks up within half an hour."

"He'll go north."

"No, he'll go south, to the city."

"He'll stay in the bush till the heat's off."

"He hasn't any food."

"He'll live off the land."

"He'll take hostages and bluff his way through."

"He'll steal a gun from somewhere and shoot it out."

"Maybe it's highly organised. Maybe someone's gonna pick him up in a helicopter or somethin'."

All the men are excited. We all want Ray Hoad to get away. It's as though he's running for us too, our representative, our champion against the screws and the whole system. And yet this escape will make it bad for us. The screws will get hard and will tighten up security in all sorts of ways. And if Ray Hoad hurts anyone while he's free, it will be very, very bad for us. The best thing for us will be if he's caught quickly before there's much publicity and before he maybe has to hurt anyone. It will be bad for the screws, too, if this thing goes on too long or if anyone gets hurt. The high-ups don't like screws who let things like this happen, and if the high-ups get savage with the screws, the screws will get even more savage with us. So we're thinking what a bastard Ray Hoad is, making it bad for us, even though we're very excited and want him to get away.

Arthur comes out of the office and is looking through the verandah wire at the lake and the bush stretching away into the distance.

"Hoad's a bloody fool, you know," he says to us, shaking his head. "He's only making trouble for everyone."

Arthur is terribly disappointed. You can see he feels hurt that Ray Hoad has done this. Ray Hoad was the pool man, the most trusted one. Arthur doesn't mention that, because he doesn't want to bring up the personal side of it, but he's very hurt.

"Did any of you know Hoad was planning to go?" he asks us. He doesn't really expect anyone to admit that they knew. He knows you can't nark on your mates. Nobody answers. You don't think that many of them knew, though you're pretty sure Bill Greene did, and maybe a couple more.

Within the hour the radio is telling about the dangerous maniac who's at large. The radio is warning people not to approach him, but to notify the police immediately. Then the radio is reporting sightings all over the place, some of them fifty miles away. It says this is the biggest manhunt in the area's history, with hundreds of police and screws involved.

Arthur is staying in the office, near the phone. Every little while a screw with a walkie-talkie comes in from the main gate to tell him how the nearest searchers are going. The ward is quiet, with all the doors locked and only a few screws left to keep watch.

We have lunch.

"I'll bet Ray's gettin' a bit faaarkin 'ungry by now," says Eddie. "Probably eatin' faaarkin witchetty grubs like a faaarkin boong."

After lunch you sit with Bill Greene and talk about Ray Hoad's chances.

"He's in an awkward position," says Bill Greene. "If he stays in the bush he won't be able to move fast, and he'll have hunger and probably exposure to cope with. The nights are bloody cold now. If he goes near a town he'll be picked up sooner or later.

His best chance was if he got a lift on the highway within the first hour or so, before the alert got into full swing."

"He might be in the city by now."

"If he's not buggered."

"Did he have any money?"

"Three dollars."

"You knew he was going?"

"Yeah."

"Why did he go, particularly?" you ask. It's a silly question. Why does anyone go?

"Well, apart from the obvious reason, he wanted to prove he could beat the cunts. You know Ray, he's not scared of anything."

You understand it. Ray Hoad is like a fox who wants to show that a fox can beat the hunters if he's clever and tough enough, and Ray is clever and tough. We're foxes too and have the fox viewpoint.

At four o'clock in the afternoon a screw calls out from the office:

"They've got him!"

"Where?" someone asks.

"About seven miles away. They're bringin' him back now."

After a while several vehicles, including a police car, come through the main gate and Ray Hoad is hauled out of one of them by screws. He looks terrible, all scratched and dirty and half fainting with weariness. He can't stand up properly, and two big screws drag him inside by his arms. They drag him down the corridor past the office and along the verandah to the cells. They're being very rough. You try to see Ray Hoad's face as he's dragged past. He looks worn out and there are cuts on his face, but he doesn't look beaten, just terribly tired. You feel proud of him for making such a good run.

He's kept locked in a cell for several weeks and nobody's allowed to see him. The screws take his meals down on trays and the meals are very small. You can imagine how hungry he must be. He's not allowed any blankets at night, just a single canvas covering and a sort of plank to sleep on. After six weeks he's brought out into the grille for a few hours each day. He's thin and starved and very pale from so long in the cell. The screws tell us we mustn't try to talk to him in the grille. Anyone caught talking to him will be locked up themselves. We manage to talk to him out of the sides of our mouths when the screws aren't looking.

"How ya goin' mate?"

"Fuckin' hungry," Ray Hoad says.

"Have the screws been biffin' ya?"

"They haven't got the fuckin' guts. They just starve a bloke."

"Yeah, the cunts," you agree.

"Listen," Ray Hoad whispers, "can ya get me somethin' to eat? A bit of bread or somethin'?"

That's awkward. It's putting you right on the spot. If the screws see you giving Ray Hoad food they'll probably lock you up. You don't want to take the risk, except that you'll feel like a weak cunt if you don't. You think how Ray Hoad wasn't afraid to take on the screws and the whole police force too, and all he's asking you to do is slip a crust through the wire.

"I'll try, mate," you whisper back.

You go back later with two slices of bread you've saved from lunch and you saunter along beside the wire of the grille. You stand side-on against the wire and swivel your eyes around to see where the screws are. Then you try to finger the two pieces of bread from your pocket through the wire and into Ray Hoad's hand. The bread is crumpled from your pocket and bits of it break off against the wire and fall on the ground.

"Shit, mate, don't waste it!" Ray Hoad whispers.

You get most of it through into his hand that he's holding down at his side, but the other pieces are still on the ground.

"Screw comin'," Ray Hoad warns you.

The screw called Smiler is walking slowly towards you. He's probably coming to warn you away from the grille. He's fifteen yards away. If you just saunter off now, as if you haven't noticed him, he might be satisfied and stop. He's far enough away that maybe he won't notice the bread on the ground if he stops where he is, but if he comes right up to the grille he'll see it for sure, and if you try to pick the bread up quickly he'll get suspicious of your sudden movement. So you start moving away from the grille very innocently, leaving the bread lying there. It works. Smiler stops and strolls back the other way. You watch from the corner of your eye, then saunter back to the grille and bend down as if you're tying your shoelace, then pick up the bits of bread and shove them quickly through to Ray. You scatter the last few crumbs with your feet. Your heart's thumping.

"Thanks, mate," Ray Hoad says. He's eating the bread by pretending to be wiping his nose with his hand.

You and Ray are pleased at how you managed it so well.

After Ray's been in the grille for a couple of weeks the screws start to relax the rule about talking to him. He's able to tell us about the escape.

"I almost didn't get over the wall. The pole was only light alloy and it was bendin' under me weight. I just got a finger grip on the top of the wall before it buckled. I was hangin' there, trying to lift meself, and thinkin' the screws 'ud see me any second. Then I managed ter shin over and dropped down on the other side. I landed off balance and I thought I'd broken me ankle. I waited a minute ter ease the pain of it, then I started through the scrub. My idea was to get to the highway pretty quick and hitch a lift out of the area before they could get organised. I skirted the lake for a coupla miles, keepin' in the scrub, knowin' I'd reach the highway sooner or later. My ankle was slowin' me up though and when I finally reached the highway, there was fuckin' cop cars goin' up and down. I knew there'd be no chance of hitchin' so I kept in the scrub, skirtin' the lake, thinkin' I might come on the railway line and maybe hop on a freight train or somethin' if one was goin' slow enough. The line must've been further than I thought. I couldn't come to it. The scrub was pretty thick and I was gettin' tired. I saw screws twice in the distance. Another time I came on two blokes choppin' wood and had to drop down quick into a blackberry bush. I felt like a friggin' pin cushion. The blokes had an old truck and I thought about tryin' ter pinch it, but it would have been tricky. They were tough lookin' cunts and might've tried to use their axes on me. I dunno whether they'd heard about the escaped maniac or not. So I went round 'em and kept goin' and got to the edge of this little town. I was gettin' sick of the scrub and I thought I'd risk goin' into the town to get some food with the coupla dollars I had. I walked up the street, hopin' I didn't look too wild with the cuts and dirt on me.

"An old lady was waterin' her front garden and she says hullo to me and starts talkin' about the weather and stuff, and about her fuckin' rheumatism. Well! I bought some bread and sausage from a shop. The shop bloke was lookin' at me a bit close, but I didn't know how far the word had spread about the escape, or whether it was on the radio or anything, so I didn't know whether the bloke was really on to me or whether he was just a fuckin' gig. There was an old deserted house at the edge of the town. It didn't have any windows and the roof was fallin' in, but I fancied it better than a night in the scrub. The afternoon was gettin' late and turnin' cold. I reckoned I should rest in the house till early next mornin' and start fresh again. To tell the truth, I was startin' ter think I'd done me dash. I should've been fifty miles away by that time. I should've been clear away. I got into the house as careful as I could and was eatin' me food when I hears cars outside. I looked out of a crack and there's screws and coppers all around. The only thing I could do was hide under a mouldy old bed and hope they'd be careless. They weren't. I see these big copper's boots walkin' up to the bed and a voice says, 'Come out from under there, you fuckin' animal!' So I stuck me head out and this young copper's pointin' his pistol at me. 'I'm gonna shoot you,' he says, real quiet. He was, too. Just then a screw comes in and tells the copper to put the pistol away. 'I'm gonna shoot this animal!' the copper says. So the screw says, real serious: 'I'm a witness. I'll see you're charged with murder!' 'I'll fuckingwell shoot you too, if you're not careful!' says the copper to the screw. 'You're a psychopath!' says the screw, and he starts yellin' for the others to come quick. About a dozen of 'em, screws and cops, come bargin' in and the young copper puts his pistol away, real sullen. Then some of 'em pulled me out from under the bed and gave me a few hits in the stomach and put me in the car. That was the end of it."

6

You are the new pool man. The most trusted one. It's a lovely job. You can go down there whenever you like and occupy yourself cleaning the filters, or sweeping the concrete surround, or working the chlorine equipment, or stacking the bags of saltash that you use with the chlorine for keeping the water healthy. The vacuuming is the most constant job. You stand on the pool side slowly working the vacuum cleaner back and forwards across the bottom, watching the suction head making clean white swathes through the even layer of dirt that gets on the pool bottom every couple of days.

The old pole has been replaced with another one, but this new one is thinner and softer alloy and couldn't possibly bear a man's weight for an instant. It's good in winter, being the pool man, because the men don't swim much and you're alone there most of the time and you don't have to worry about keeping the PH level of the water exact. You just keep everything looking clean.

Your mother has sent you a little pocket radio and you can stand there slowly vacuuming on cool, sunny days listening to classical music or thinking about poetry. You don't have to worry much about your lip movements down here because you are alone most of the time and, anyway, you're the most trusted one now and the screws don't bother reporting every little thing about you any more. They all know you're interested in poetry and they make allowance for you being a bit peculiar.

You've written a poem that's been published. That made a lot of difference. The screws think that writing a poem and getting it published means you're an intellectual or something. It was only a small poem that began:

"The sky lies in puddles
Like pieces of a dropped plate"

The rest of it wasn't as good as those first lines, but it got published, and seeing it in print in the magazine made you so happy and proud you felt like bursting. It was Marian's doing. You've been exchanging little notes with her each week when the batches of library books are sent back and forth. She would ask you about your reading and you'd write back and tell her your thoughts about Thomas Hardy or John Galsworthy or someone like that. Then she asked whether you were writing any poems, and asked to be allowed to see some of them perhaps. After the first shyness you sent her a few of your poems, very afraid she'd think them stupid and silly. But she didn't, she liked them. So you kept trying to write more, so you'd have new things to send to Marian.

"Have you thought about publication?" Marian had asked in one of her notes. Of course, you hadn't. Only real poets get published. But Marian kept on about publication, even saying once that she would get angry with you if you didn't try to get your poems into print. And so, because you'd rather die than have Marian angry, you sent a poem to a magazine she told you about. It came back with a rejection slip and a message from the editor in mauve coloured pencil on the bottom, saying you should keep trying. The next one came back too, and the next one, and all the others for months. You were a bit uneasy about sending poems out in your mail, wondering what Arthur would think. Arthur or one of the other screws read all the men's outgoing mail to make sure they aren't writing insane things or threatening or frightening anyone.

"Er, is it all right for me to be sending poems to magazines?" you'd asked him.

He'd looked at you, pursing his lips.

"Oh, I suppose there's no harm in it," he'd said. "Of course it depends on the subject matter of them."

"How do you mean?"

"Well, obviously we can't allow you to send anything that slanders the hospital or the staff. As long as you only write what's fair and balanced, it's all right. For instance, if you use a phrase like 'the shabby walls' to describe the ward it would be acceptable, but, say, descriptions of men being beaten, that's going too far. That sort of thing might bring some reprisal."

You got the message, especially the part about "reprisal". You got that part very clearly. And you know what a screw means when he talks about "slander". One day after that, Arthur had said to you: "The doctor liked that poem of yours, about the magpie."

"Really?"

"Yes, I showed it to him. He was very impressed. He's very pleased with you generally."

That was good news. To have the doctor very pleased with you generally means the shock and medication are a comfortable way off. It means you've got room to manoeuvre, but not too much, of course. You mustn't get too secure.

So you sent the poem about the sky like a dropped plate and a note came back in the mauve coloured pencil telling you it was accepted. Marian was terribly glad about it.

"I TOLD YOU SO!" she wrote. The word "told" was underlined six times. Then one day a copy of the thin little magazine came, compliments of the editor, and there was your poem on page twenty-nine.

You think you're in love with Marian. You dwell on her all the time, on her long beautiful legs and brown hair and lovely smile and on the little swell at the front of her jumper that you remember from the time you talked to her in the office. Often, when you're alone, you take out one of her notes and kiss the neat handwriting that she did with her slim, smooth fingers. You think of her frantically at night in the cell, when you know you won't be able to sleep until you pull yourself and have a climax. The best climaxes come from thinking about Marian.

Sam Lister has a beautiful wife who visits him. Sam's wife is almost as beautiful as Marian, but of course not quite. Sometimes Sam invites you to sit with them in the visiting room. They talk together in a lovely soft way, about what she's been doing, the films she's seen, the friends she's bumped into lately, or about her job as a secretary. She's waiting very patiently for Sam to be free again. You think what hell it must be for Sam to be away from her. It's very painful when she has to go. You can feel the pain of it passing between them and Sam has a desperate look for hours afterwards.

Smiler the screw has started persecuting Sam Lister. We don't know why. Smiler doesn't have reasons for anything, he's just the way he is. He finds fault with whatever Sam does, and keeps reporting him to Arthur. He snaps and snarls at Sam, hoping to goad him into some reaction to punish him for. The worst time for Sam is when Smiler's on night duty. Smiler comes banging on the cell door all night, so that Sam can't sleep. After four or five nights of this Sam begins to break down with the strain. Today Sam dropped a scrap of paper on the verandah. Smiler snarled at him, saying he was a filthy, messy pig, then grabbed Sam's arm and marched him down the verandah and made him pick the paper up and put it in the bin. Sam hasn't slept properly for weeks now and he stumbled and overbalanced while Smiler was holding him. Smiler pretended that Sam was getting violent. He shoved Sam against the wall hard and then punched him. The screw kept smiling. He always smiles. That's why they gave him the nickname.

Now Sam is in Arthur's office, protesting about the persecution. His nerves are making him shake and he's crying. The shaking and crying will make it seem as though he's mentally ill and needs shock or medication. Everyone knows that mentally ill people think they're being persecuted, so Sam is sealing his own fate by accusing Smiler. Smiler is pleased at how beautifully it's working out.

You watch these things happening, feeling that you should be writing about them in poems, writing about the real things here, the bad things, the way Wilfred Owen or Siegfried Sassoon wrote about the bad things they saw.

But you know they'd call it "slander".

It's hot summer weather again, just like it was when you came here. The sky stays very blue day after day, and the vegetable gardens are full of green things growing, with a mist of spray over them from sprinklers. You're vacuuming the pool, leaning a little on the pole and gazing up to where the top of the wall meets the sky. There are some birds sitting there watching you. Some little brown finches are darting near your head, going back and forth from the rafters of the shed beside the pool where the chlorine equipment is. They nest in the rafters. A warm, soft breeze is brushing your skin. A breeze full of lovely smells, smells of earth and green things growing, and of hot brick wall, and of flowers and eucalypts and a small acrid whiff of chlorine to give the mingled smells a sharpness. Someone is calling out, asking Mario about the gardening.

"Mario, you mad wog, we water this bed? Yes?"

"Issa good!" Mario calls back.

Other men and screws are talking among themselves and making a low buzz of voices that floats across like the buzzing of summer insects.

You think you should be happy. Life seems very easy right now, with the summer weather and the nice pressure of the vacuum pole against you and you being the pool man and the trusted one. You should feel happy because Marian is coming to see you for another talk. She's told you so in one of her notes. You should be grateful because Arthur has made you the trusted one and because Electric Ned says he's very pleased with you. Yesterday he told you that you'd made a good start in your first year here. You should be grateful too because none of the screws bother you much in a bad way any more, not even Smiler. If you chose, you could go on having it easy, being the trusted one, and the longer you went on the easier it would get. In a couple more years your position would be very secure, and the good reports would be accumulating in your file, so that maybe after a few years they'd start thinking about transferring you to the open section. A few years isn't long. Men have been transferred after only a few years. Yes, you could have it easy if you play your cards right and a bit of luck is with you.

Now we are having Christmas dinner. All of us at a long table on the verandah. The long table is made from the dining room tables laid end to end and covered with sheets. On the table are soft drinks and potato chips and plates full of peanuts and sweets. There's a little coloured party hat at each man's place, but nobody's wearing them, except a few men like Barry Clarke. A screw put the hat on Barry and tied it with the elastic under his chin and Barry's too doped with medication to care.

The screws serve up chicken, then plum pudding. After the main eating is finished, Arthur makes a little speech, wishing us a merry Christmas and thanking us for being so good during the year. He says it makes his job easy, having such a decent bunch of chaps to look after.

Then one of the men stands up and wishes Arthur and the other screws merry Christmas and thanks them for putting on such a lovely dinner.

You just keep looking at the tablecloth while the speeches are happening. You look across at Sam Lister. Sam's had shock treatment. His eyes are vacant and he doesn't know where he is. A screw has been feeding him the chicken and plum pudding, guiding spoonful by spoonful between his slack lips. The screw puts a party hat on him. It's a red one with little spangles and it sits up on the top of his head.

Eddie comes out of the office. He's wearing a Santa Claus suit and carrying a bag of presents. He goes round the table, handing each man a little package in coloured paper. He's trying to be jolly.

"Here's a faaarkin present for ya!" he says to you. You unwrap it. There are two ballpoint pens and a packet of cigarettes. The screws have tried to make each present fit the individual, so they've given you pens to write your poems with.

You sit staring at the tablecloth, thinking you're going to die of sorrow.

THE CURE

*"Imagination and memory are but one thing,
which for divers considerations hath divers names."*

HOBBES

1

You've arrived, and had the standard pep-talk from the Charge, and now you're sitting on the verandah trying to keep the exact mixture of expressions on your face to show gladness and gratitude and a few other things. You mustn't let it look like an act. It must look like your true feelings coming out, as if the last thing on your mind is that screws might be observing you. Then you get worried that maybe you're being too passive. A mentally well person would take an interest in new surroundings. So you stroll halfway down the yard and gaze about, taking care not to seem too interested in the fence. The fence is just wire netting with a single strand of barbs on top.

You can see into the yard of Ward 5 on the left where some old women are wandering as if deep in thought, or as though they're looking for something they've lost. And you can see into Ward 7 on the other side. There are wheelchairs parked on a scrap of lawn and figures slumped in them with shining strings of spit hanging from their mouths. There are mongols too, retarded patients, little monkeyish boys who rush about, or stare at the sky, or pick at their bodies as if they've just discovered that they have bodies. One is clinging naked and upside down on the fence. Ward 7 looks bad, as though THE END was written across it invisibly. Of course all the wards are like that and you always want to think some other ward is worse than your own.

Down in front is a dirt road with nurses' cars parked, and beyond a wooden building with the noise of something like a power saw coming out of it and half-finished baskets piled around the entrance. A sign says Occupational Therapy. Past the wooden building you can see vegetable gardens and then a row of willow trees and then a big swampy pond. A long way away to the right are some buildings set among trees. The biggest of them has a boxy shape and might be the hall. Another could be the library. It has a sign on it that you can't quite read, but the sign has the right number of letters to say Library. Someone comes out with what are probably books under her arm. You hear the faint squeak of the flyscreen door and then the bang when it shuts. You feel a slight flutter in your stomach, thinking how that person could have been Marian. Marian used to be the hospital librarian and you used to be in love with her. But Marian left long ago. The building next to the library is small and without windows. The sign has the right number of letters to say Morgue.

That's about all you can see from here. You could perhaps see a bit more from the bottom of the yard, but you don't dare go that far yet. The screws are watching your first reactions and especially your reaction to the flimsy netting with its one strand of barbs. You half imagine screws crouched inside, like runners on their starting-blocks, ready to sprint out and grab you if you approach the fence too eagerly. Nearly five years in maximum security—the place they call MAX—have made high brick walls and whole thickets of barbed wire seem proper. This feels like a mistake.

Everyone in MAX dreams of a transfer here. It can be the first step to eventual release and only about one in ten ever makes it. You're remembering how you shook hands with blokes whose transfers had come through, dying with envy, wondering what it'd be like to crack the one-in-ten lottery with the single ticket that cost years to buy. And after the Charge was killed with a pitchfork by mad old Lubecki you'd begged God to get you out of MAX. It was very bad after the killing. The screws acted as though we'd all had a hand in it, which wasn't fair. You can sort of understand, though, that they didn't feel much like being fair. Ray Hoad and Bill Greene wanted to have a wreath sent from all of us and you argued against it, not because you didn't agree with showing respect but you were afraid it might be taken the wrong way. Flowers from the culprits. The screws finally allowed the wreath, on condition it was anonymous.

Now you're here and you just feel lost and lonely. There are too many possibilities here, though you don't know yet what they are. In MAX there were so few possibilities, but you knew them exactly; they fitted tight around your life like the high walls. Even this stretch of dirt road seems too much. The road comes from somewhere and goes somewhere and the world—or bits of the world—travel past. There was nothing in MAX to remind you of the world coming and going and so you got used to living in a kind of stillness that you only really sense now you're out of it. There isn't that stillness here, even though it's a quiet afternoon with little happening. You'll never have that stillness in your life again. Unless you make a cock-up and get sent back.

Except for some of the screws there isn't a single face you know. A few men are lying on the grass. A few more are sitting on the verandah or pacing along the fence. They mostly wear baggy grey hospital-issue and look like dills. A dill is a patient who's too mad or stupid to know what's going on and you can never be mates with a dill because you can't rely on him. These are scrapings from other chronic or retard wards, put here for being especially difficult or disturbed. Refractory types, which is why this ward is called REFRACT. They're here as a punishment and that alone sets them apart from someone like you who had to sweat years to get here. Two or three men are going in and out of the pantry door, wearing aprons and banging dixies and fooling about. You don't know them or what routines they are following. In MAX you'd know everything. Knowing everything kept you safe.

A very small bandy-legged bloke is circling the yard. He has a thin sharp face. On one of his rounds he veers across to you.

"Gettin' out Tuesday!" he declares.

"That's good," you say.

"Yep, Tuesday's the day!"

"Terrific."

He stands grinning at you and rubbing his hands with glee. He does another round of the yard. As he passes you again you give him a friendly look.

"What are you giggin' at, ya fuckin' mongrel-eyed hoon?" he yells, shoving his sharp face at you.

"Nothing," you say quickly.

"Ya slimy cunt!" he screams. "I'll fuckinwell knock ya rotten!"

"Sorry mate," you say. He's too small to be afraid of, but you don't want any trouble. And you don't know what game this bloke's playing, if he is playing. He glares savagely for another moment and stalks off. When he comes by you again you stare in the opposite direction. He stops in a friendly way and tells you about Tuesday. His mind is gone.

You think you've got this little dill measured. There are sixty men in REFRACT. Fifty-nine measures to get.

The afternoon is turning colder and the shadow of the ward is beginning to go across the dirt road. Some men come up from the vegetable garden and stand at the gate in the fence. A couple more come from Occupational Therapy, and a few more from other directions. A screw unlocks and they troop in. You see Fred Henderson. He was in MAX and got his transfer a year ago. He's about fifty, red-faced, and wheezes a lot. You were never real friends with him because he was out of your age group. Besides, Fred Henderson was always a bit chummy with the screws, playing cards with them and helping them take the mickey out of patients. You and Bill Greene and Ray Hoad made fun of patients too, but only amongst yourselves.

"I heard you was comin' over," says Fred Henderson.

It's just like him to have "heard".

He wants to hear the latest from MAX, mainly about blokes he made fun of. You tell him how so-and-so was caught sucking-off in the shower and he has a good wheeze at that. You laugh with him. Fred Henderson lowers his voice.

"Some of the screws aren't too happy with your transfer," he says.

"Why not?" you ask. You never know with Fred Henderson whether he's giving you a helpful tip or taking a rise out of you or fishing for something to tell his pals.

"They reckon you're still psychotic," he says.

"Yeah?" you say. You mustn't make the mistake of denying it. By the time the story got back to the screws it may sound as though you are denying there's anything wrong with you at all, and that's the mark of a troublemaker.

You start changing the subject, asking about the routine here.

You see Dennis Lane come to the gate and then inside. Dennis Lane was the best ping-pong player in MAX. Ping-pong was the only thing you ever associated him with. He was very quiet, with a brooding self-control. He hadn't many brilliant shots, just a perfect defensive game. You wave to Dennis Lane and he glances back and walks up inside the ward. If it was anyone else you'd think something was wrong, but this is just Dennis Lane's manner.

Suddenly there's a commotion and a black man bounds down the yard, blubbering around Fred Henderson, pawing him like a big silly dog.

"Bimbo, you black bastard!" Fred Henderson shouts, and slaps the man's head. "Shake hands with Len," he orders. Bimbo stares wide-eyed at you. He seems to have a fixed idea.

"Willee root me?" he keeps asking. "Willee root me, eh? Willee, eh? Willee root me?"

"Bloody oath he will!" Fred Henderson tells him, winking at you. You put your hand out to Bimbo and Fred Henderson punches him in the ribs to make him shake.

"Show Len the war dance!" Fred Henderson orders. Bimbo capers for you and does a chant with his big lips spitting and flapping until another punch stops him. Bimbo squats at Fred Henderson's feet. He points to other men in the yard and babbles.

"Dat one root me? Willee, eh? Wot 'bout dat one? Willee root me, eh?" Fred Henderson kicks him to shut him up.

"I'm the black bugger's best friend," says Fred Henderson.

The Charge shouts from the verandah for us to come inside. Screws are locking the outer doors of the ward. Some of the grey figures on the grass have to be prodded. The little bandy-legged man is hurling abuse at a screw trying to shepherd him.

"I'll knock you into the middle of next week!" the screw threatens.

Make it Tuesday, you mutter.

The dining room is long and shabby and lit by bare lights that give a lurid effect. Ten large tables are set in two rows. A screw motions you to a place near Dennis Lane. The tables are graded. The end ones in the other row are for the worst dills. Bimbo is there with a monstrous hunchback and a whole bunch of others who are gibbering, or twisting about, or lolling vacantly. A servery rolls open at the end of the room and plates are pushed through. The men rise from the tables by turns, bumping and stumbling, to collect the food. Those at the worst tables are snuffling the meal down, or mashing it on the table, or treading it into the floor. The scene is unsettling after the orderliness of MAX. You glance at the screws but they don't seem bothered. Then seconds are called. This too is strange. They almost never allowed seconds in MAX. They kept you hungry on principle. Bimbo goes for seconds and a screw piles the plate high and when that's finished insists on giving him another lot. A dessert of jelly is next and seconds are called again. Bimbo is plied with three helpings, then four. After the sixth he's had enough, but the screw swears to skin his hide unless he eats more. Bimbo's half-laughing and half-choking. Finally he vomits on the table and a cheer goes up.

"He's finished," says the screw and heaves the rest into a bin.

After tea some of the men go upstairs to bed. The others crowd into the dayroom to watch TV or play cards or snooker or just sprawl in chairs. The dayroom quickly fills with smoke and the smells of so many men. You walk out on the wired-in side section of the verandah where the Charge's office is. The screws are gathered in there, waiting to go home. They notice you and say something among themselves. You wish you hadn't wandered out here. You'd rather not attract attention. Past the office is a row of rooms for a few of the better patients, the silvertails. Fred Henderson has one. They're really cells, with the heavy doors that cells have, but these are called rooms and aren't locked. You stroll along near the rooms and stand in shadow. It's quieter here, and cool. The moon is coming up over the tiled roof opposite, making the tiles gleam silver.

The day-screws begin to go and the night-screws arrive. You get tense when you see the senior night-screw is Smiler, an old enemy. You think you should go back and lose yourself a bit among the other men, but it wouldn't help. Smiler knows you're here. That's the first thing they'd tell him.

Smiler comes from the office. He's smiling of course. He always smiles. He says how glad he is that you got this transfer. He says he always would've bet money on you getting it sooner or later. He starts telling you that the essence of this ward is trust, and he even spells it for you: T-R-U-S-T. The security here is a sham, he says, and any bloke can piss off if he wants to. Smiler describes a few methods of escape and how a bloke could hitch a lift on the highway and be in the city in two hours.

"I'm a sportsman," he says. "I'll give anyone a head start. I'll even unlock the door."

All the while you are giving him a steady man-to-man look, as though you're full of quiet respect for a straight-talking fellow. Smiler strolls off and you return to the smoke and smell of the dayroom. You'd rather stay in the cool shadows and watch the moon, but it seems spoiled.

At ten o'clock we are herded upstairs. You enter a huge dormitory that looks like a flophouse, with rickety iron beds packed close together. The junior screw consults a bed plan and tells you 43 is yours, then he and Smiler go out and you hear keys in the lock. The big room is draughty and cold. You sit on your bed and examine an old pair of pyjamas that are there. They've been washed but the pants have the remains of a shit stain and a faint smell of it. The dormitory lights are switched off from somewhere outside. Your bed is against the wall near a window. You are very pleased about that. Half the knack of survival is getting near windows.

You undress to your singlet and roll the clothes into a tight bundle, then put your valuables inside the bundle. There's your comb, your toothbrush, your two-dollar note which you can't spend but which is nice to have, your pad with scribbled bits of poems, your biro, and your transistor radio. The radio is your prized possession. It's so small it can go in your shirt pocket and it has given you some wonderful times. You learned to like classical music from this little radio. Some of the best times in MAX were when you were working in the vegetable garden or taking care of the swimming pool and the sun and wind and birdsong all around made you feel really happy; then you could tune your shirt pocket to some classical music and the happiness was complete. You got fresh batteries on the weekly buy-up when they let you order a dollar's worth of stuff from the canteen. Most blokes ordered tobacco, but you spent your buy-up on biros and note-pads and Sao biscuits and batteries. You wonder how you'll get those things now. You suppose they have weekly buy-ups here too.

You put the bundle under the bed and hop between the covers. You lie for a while, feeling how hard the mattress is and trying to sort out the smells in it. Then you decide you'd better keep your bundle closer so you take it into the bed. By turning your head upwards you can see out of the top of the window to where some trees are tossing in a wind. You can't hear the wind so the tossing seems more to be in time with the sighing and snoring of the men in the dormitory.

A dark figure is moving between the beds. It's Bimbo, naked, his long penis hanging down. He is shoved away from several beds before someone opens the blankets for him and he gets in. You see them moving under the blankets and hear the old iron bed squeak to the rhythm. You hug yourself, trying not to giggle too loud. You wish Ray Hoad and Bill Greene were here. What a joke they'd make of it!

2

Mornings are good in REFRACT, mainly because it's so good to leave the stuffy smell of the dormitory. There's always a lot of banging and bustle when the day-screws unlock the door and barge in shouting, "Hands off cocks! On socks!" the way they do. You wash your face and clean your teeth at a basin, shave with a locked razor, then go down into the yard.

It's autumn weather. The mornings are cool and sunny and the yard looks fresh, the sun at a changed angle and the ground wet with dew. You can't know a place until you've seen it at all times of the day and in all weathers and all seasons. It takes a year. The sun shines on the big pond at this time of morning. It shines on the water and on the trees and on the tin roof of Occupational Therapy. The tin roof looks like a sheet of flowing water all lit up, with the pond another sheet of water down lower behind it, as if the pond is being filled by the flow of the tin.

You are used to the fence now. You go down to it and look through at the few things you couldn't see the first day. There isn't much more—just a few extra trees and a curve of the dirt road where it goes up past a row of wards slightly raised on a ridge far off to the left. You watch the morning routine, fixing more details in your mind. Some men are doing chores. The dayroom chairs are carried out to the lawn so the dayroom can be swept and polished, then they are put back. You lend a hand, to show you aren't a bludger.

Fred Henderson and a couple of screws are playing crib at a table outside the Charge's office. Fred Henderson calls to you to join in and you have to say you don't know crib. For a moment you wish you did. You could get in with the screws, be one of their card-playing circle. It would ease your way here. Then you realise it's a silly idea. You need a personality like Fred Henderson's to get in with screws. You'd need to be able to stay loud and hearty all the time and mock everything and go on endlessly about cars and football and sheilas. There'd be no time to think your own thoughts. In MAX you were able to mock and joke and be stupid with your mates because with them it was deliberate. It was like farting at the system, or like keeping a ball in the air. The screws don't even know there's a ball. They think they're normal.

After breakfast men go off to work-places, clumping in boots. You sit around in the yard until lunch and see them all come back. It's the same in the afternoon. You don't seem expected to do anything so you just watch the others in the yard. The little bandy-legged bloke has told you about Tuesday at least a hundred times and has abused you a lot more also. And there is an old bloke who sits gobbing stuff out of his throat all day long and yelling, "Burn me alive, damn you! Burn me alive!" And there's a tall epileptic named Harris who is supposed to be a king-hit merchant. He will come over and start talking and you notice him edging a bit closer to you than he needs to, so you edge away. If he goes on talking to you for a while you find you've both edged halfway across the yard. And there is somebody called Silas Throgmorton sick in one of the rooms. The screws keep taking him cups of tea and medicine. They seem fond of him. Whenever screws go in the room you hear an old sick voice declaring something about being The Owner and The Maker and threatening to sack the whole bloody crew unless they smarten up. And there is Dunn, a thin lanky bloke with a ratty moustache. Dunn strides about sneering when he hears the sick old voice from the room.

"Bah, Frogmorton? I had my first fifty billion before that bastard was born!"

Small bands of patients go past on the dirt road, mostly retards of both sexes and usually with a female nurse. They wander along gradually getting all out of step and lagging like sheep until the group is strung out along the road. The nurse will stop and call for the stragglers, or will go back and shoo them forward, and then they all pass out of sight. A while later they come back in the opposite direction and you see the straggling and shepherding happen again. You still aren't used to seeing female nurses.

There are female nurses in the wards alongside. Pretty girls in blue uniforms. And there are some in Occupational Therapy. One in particular often comes out to pick up or put down half-finished baskets near the door. You see her now. She's slim and nice, with brown hair tied back. She takes a basket and turns to go in, then pauses and looks across towards you. She's just having a stickybeak into the yard you suppose. You try to see her face clearly. Yes, she's nice. You suddenly realise she might be looking at *you*. It makes you want to shrink away to nothing. You get a picture of what she's seeing if she is looking at you. She's seeing a dill in baggy rags and a rough haircut, someone she wouldn't want to touch because he's probably smelly and has dribble on him. You close your eyes, wishing she'd go inside, and when you open them after a moment she is gone. You feel like crying. You mutter, "Stuck-up bitch!" a few times and it helps the crying feeling go away. In a little while you are able to tell yourself that it was a good thing to have happened because there was a lesson in it. Lessons arm you if you learn them properly and early. The lesson this time is that female nurses can do something that male screws can't. They can shame you.

Later in the afternoon you are strolling by the bottom fence. The grass is in the shadow of the ward and too cold now to sit on. You sense a tension around the Charge's office. The Charge is on the phone. He comes out to confer with other screws, then talks again on the phone. You stay near the fence, keeping out of whatever it might be, but glancing at the screws to see if they are looking your way. If this tension concerns you they'd be looking. You don't seem to be on their minds, which means you need not be really scared, just nervous in a general way. You can still suffer from the fallout of someone else's trouble, if it's bad, but you'll survive.

Dennis Lane comes along the dirt road to the gate in the fence and stands in his brooding, self-controlled way, waiting to be let in. He's early. You half-think to walk across and talk to him through the fence while he's waiting, tip him off about the tension. Then a screw on the verandah notices Dennis and calls something to the Charge in the office. The screw walks down briskly with his key at the ready, but as though he wants to appear to be acting quite routinely until Dennis Lane is safely through the gate. You know who the tension is about.

Dennis Lane is taken into the Charge's office and you glimpse him behind the glass. He's sitting, with screws around him. The Charge gets on the phone again. The men arrive back from the work-places. Just before tea a screw brings a suitcase and puts it down outside the office. It's Dennis Lane's gear. He's going back to MAX. Screws bring Dennis Lane out of the office. He looks just as he always did when you faced him along the ping-pong table and he patiently hit every ball back until you felt you were playing against a wall. He is put in a car and driven away.

Fred Henderson has the details.

"Silly bastard was doin' his balls over some retard bitch from Ward 12. This afternoon he caught 'er at the canteen with a little boyfriend she 'ad on the side. Dennis did his block. Threatened to cut 'er throat. Anyway, that's what our Charge was told, and 'e got it from the Charge of 12 who got it from the canteen manager who got it from the girl on the counter."

Fred Henderson hasn't much sympathy.

"Well fuck me dead! Dennis was 'ere in the first place for cuttin' 'is missus's throat! How many throats does 'e reckon 'e's allowed?"

It's true. Dennis Lane has been worse than stupid, worse than idiotic. You can't think of a word to describe it, except maybe "mad", and you learned long ago that that word doesn't mean anything. It took Dennis Lane nine years to get his transfer. He might get another in nine more. He'll have plenty of time to search for the appropriate word, and to polish his defensive game.

"You're no longer a man of leisure," the Charge tells you one morning. "You're to start at OT today."

"Righto!" you say, trying to sound keen. You aren't sure whether you are keen or not. You've begun to be used to staying in the yard all day, watching the other men there and the activity along the dirt road, learning how the sun looks on the trees and grass, knowing the time by the shadows.

And there's your reading . . .

You've been able to get your two most precious books from among your few bits of gear in the storeroom. You had to choose carefully because there are no lockers here, no place to keep private things safe, so you must carry them with you the whole time. And the screws get irritated if you ask them to unlock the storeroom too often. You chose your anthology of poems, the lovely green-covered book your mother got you and from which you first understood about poetry. The other choice was a novel you discovered a year ago. This novel had become part of your life, or maybe part of your life had entered the novel —it was hard to say which. Finding it was like an act of fate. A poet wrote to you after you'd had a piece of verse published in a little magazine. You wrote back and for a while the two of you became quite friends. The poet wrote very good letters, full of quotations from Shakespeare, and how his wounded spirit ached for sanctuary, things like that. He told you that you simply *must* read *The Survivor*. The poet was always telling you that you simply must do this or that—read Proust, take Vitamin B, learn chess. A lot of the suggestions didn't seem to have much connection with your life in MAX, but when he said about *The Survivor*, and told you the outline, you really wanted to get hold of it. It was about a person called David Allison who has an unhappy childhood, then goes to the trenches in Flanders, and afterwards tries to become a writer so as to tell the truth of the war for the sake of all the dead men. The story seemed, from what the poet told you, to connect with a lot of your own thoughts and feelings. A few months later you were helping clean out the cell old Tom Hawksworth had had for forty years. You found some mouldy books and one of them was *The Survivor*! You could barely believe it. The copy was torn and the last few pages were missing but that didn't matter. You hid it quickly under your jacket and kept it. Old Tom Hawksworth was dead, so he didn't care.

The anthology and the wonderful novel are probably the only two books you'll ever need in your life. Between them they seem able to tell you everything you'll ever need to know or understand. But Occupational Therapy is a whole new situation and you'd rather not have to face a whole new situation just yet.

Peter Kocan

On the other hand you will be in REFRACT for several years and you can't stay sitting in the yard for that long. You weigh the pros and cons of going to Occupational Therapy, then you remember that no-one's asking your opinion anyway.

"This is the doctor's brainwave, not mine," grumbles the Charge as he unlocks the gate in the fence after breakfast. The Charge doesn't like you being let out to work. He doesn't like you staying idle in the yard either. His remark about being a man of leisure had an edge to it. All he'd like is for you to be back in MAX.

You step through the gate and wait for him. He just waves you irritably on. "Go along. I'll sight you," he says. "Sighting" is when a screw watches you go somewhere. You walk on, feeling strange. This is the first time in nearly five years that you've been outside walls and fences without a screw next to you. You walk in a very straight line so the Charge won't think you are turning off to bolt. When you get to the door of OT you turn to wave, feeling grateful that you've been trusted a little bit, but the Charge is already going up the yard with his back turned. He probably doesn't care if you escape now—it'd be the doctor's fault.

Inside the door the noise of a power saw is very loud and the air's thick with pine-smelling dust. A dozen or so men are handling tools and machines and lengths of wood. You stand wondering what to do. A couple of screws are working with the men and you can see the brown-haired nurse through another door. Nobody takes any notice of you. You ask a man where the boss is. He can't hear you properly. You shout in his ear and he shrugs. One of the screws comes past with a long plank, forcing you out of the way.

The brown-haired nurse comes through the room carrying a basket.

"Did you want something?" she asks, leaning close so you'll hear.

"I was sent from REFRACT."

"Oh, are you Tarbutt?"

"Yes."

100

She looks at you with wide blue eyes, as though being Tarbutt is the last thing she expected of you. You can't bring yourself to return her gaze directly but you try not to seem too shifty, or too aware of her body.

"You'll have to see Mr Trowbridge," she tells you, and leads the way into a rough office littered with wood and paint pots and pieces of metal and other things. Mr Trowbridge is the Charge here, though his title is Therapy Supervisor or something. He's a tall man about fifty. He has a stooped, moody look, and an air of being preoccupied with ten different problems so that you only have about a tenth of his attention.

"Your ward doctor recommends you highly," says Mr Trowbridge. "I wouldn't normally take someone so recently out of MAX." The noise is still loud from the work room and you have to strain to hear. Mr Trowbridge abruptly goes out to help someone align a drill, then gets caught up with several other jobs, then comes back.

"Well, what d'you fancy doing?" he asks.

"I'm not sure," you answer. You would like to say you won't be able to bear the constant noise. The noise is like it was in the factory you worked in when you were free. When you were going mad. "We need someone for our vinyl bag section. Can you use a sewing machine?" he asks.

"No."

"Come and have a look."

You follow through the dust and noise to the rear of the building. There's a big bank of windows that face across the vegetable gardens to the willow trees and the pond. At one end of a long room are patients doing basketwork with the brown-haired nurse. At the other end is a corner full of stacked rolls of vinyl, a table, a tool-rack, and a large, ancient sewing machine.

"This is the old girl," Mr Trowbridge says, whipping a cover off the machine. "Manufactured 1922. Treadle type originally. As you see, we've electrified it."

He shows you a vinyl bag.

"This is the finished item."

It's a proper ladies' shopping bag with handles and a front pocket and metal clasps. It looks hard to make.

"This is how you thread and operate the machine."

Mr Trowbridge sits down and quickly runs the thread from the top spool down through a series of hooks and loops into the needle, then he brings the thread up from a spool underneath. Then he takes a piece of scrap vinyl and sews across it very fast about twenty times. You can't follow any of this.

"The cutting is done this way."

He spreads a roll of vinyl on the table and begins marking it with a set of plywood patterns.

"The main thing's to use the vinyl economically. It's expensive."

Mr Trowbridge has marked a full set of patterns when he is called away.

"Right. Cut out the pieces, then try to work out how they should be sewn together, using the finished bag as a model. I'll check on your progress later."

Mr Trowbridge goes.

You take a pair of heavy scissors from the rack and slowly cut the vinyl. After you have looked at the cut pieces for a long time, comparing them with the parts of the finished bag, you think you see how they go. You wonder when Mr Trowbridge will return to teach you the sewing. But maybe he meant for you to just go ahead. Maybe he was teaching you the sewing when he zipped across the scrap vinyl twenty times. Maybe he assumes you now know all about it. You sit there, trying to think exactly what he said before he went, but the more you think about it the more confusing it seems. If you go ahead and try to sew you might get into trouble for doing something you weren't told to do. If you don't go ahead you may be in trouble for not doing what you were told.

You're always like this. That's partly how you know you aren't the same as most people. Most people just see one meaning and go ahead and it turns out okay. The only other person you know of who thinks and thinks and worries and worries like you is David Allison in *The Survivor*. That's why you often feel that David Allison is your only friend, almost the only real person you know.

After a long time you go to ask Mr Trowbridge what he meant. He's pushing a length of timber through a planing machine which makes the worst noise you've ever heard. You shout to make him hear, then you get too close and nudge the timber so that it goes crooked in the machine. Mr Trowbridge yells at you to get back to the vinyl section and he'll attend to you when he's ready.

You decide you should try to sew. You put a scrap of vinyl under the needle and press the treadle. There is a burst of electricity, the vinyl whizzes through, and the machine stops in a big tangle of thread. You spend a minute recovering from the fright, then try to unpick the tangle. You can't figure how to rethread through all the hooks and loops. You try a few different ways but the tangle happens again when you touch the treadle.

Mr Trowbridge returns and shows you the threading again and when he goes away you mess it up. You have to sit there as if you are really keen to understand how it works, as if you are thinking the problem out, but you know you can't because you are too stupid.

You have sensed the brown-haired nurse glancing at you from time to time from the basket section. You haven't dared glance back except a couple of times quickly. There is another nurse who is slightly older and more senior and who is Mr Trowbridge's deputy. The noise isn't as bad here, and there's a lull sometimes, so the two nurses do a lot of talking and joking between themselves and with their patients. They even have a gramophone and play records during the lulls in the noise. You learn from the talk that the brown-haired nurse is Cheryl and the senior one is Janice.

"What music do you like?" Janice asks you.

"Oh, any," you say, surprised at being spoken to.

"Ronnie & the Roundabouts?"

"They're alright," you say.

"We're all crazy about Ronnie & the Roundabouts here," Janice says. "Except *her*," she adds, pointing at Cheryl. "And she doesn't matter."

"That's no way to talk about a lady," says an old bloke in a wheelchair. He seems to act as Janice's straight man.

"That's no lady! That's Cheryl!"

Cheryl grins and pretends to hit Janice with a basket. There's this constant banter about Cheryl being a bit of a fool who doesn't matter. She doesn't appear to mind and she occasionally gets her own back with a wisecrack. All the same, you wish you hadn't said you liked Ronnie & the Roundabouts. You're on Cheryl's side.

It's odd to have the rack of tools near you. It holds knives, awls, scissors—dangerous things. In MAX you were treated as a maniac who couldn't be trusted with a knife and fork to eat with. Of course there were inconsistencies—no knives in the dining room but hoes and pitchforks in the garden. You don't look at these tools much. You don't want to seem too interested in them. You notice, though, that the pliers have had the wire-cutting parts filed out.

The day drags along to four o'clock. You've done nothing but sit glumly at a machine you can't fathom. Mr Trowbridge has shown you how to thread several times now, getting moodier and more silent each time. He has probably decided you're a dud. He might even think you are acting this way on purpose—a psychotic's devious method of asking to go home to MAX. They say madmen often signal in behaviour what they can't say in words.

Mr Trowbridge escorts you back to the ward, telling you on the way that you'll need to pull your socks up. A quarter of an hour later the Charge calls you to the office.

"I've had a call from OT. An awl is missing."

You don't say anything.

"Have you got it?"

"No."

"I'll have to search you."

"Alright."

Later he tells you it's been found at OT.

3

Silas Throgmorton has recovered slightly, perhaps because of all the cups of tea the screws have taken him. You are on the verandah one Sunday morning, reading a little, listening to your transistor radio which you keep tuned low so the classical music won't offend anybody.

"I'M THE OWNER AND THE MAKER!"

You look up. An old man is standing there. He has a blanket round his shoulders like a robe and is wearing a tall hat with a ribbon of toilet paper tied to it and trailing down his back. He looks like a king.

"It's all mine!" he shouts, staring at the ward and the yard and everything else within view.

Dunn is in the yard. He whirls round, tugging at his ratty moustache.

"Bah! Rubbish! It's MINE!"

"Hand it over to me!" the king shouts, pointing a bony finger at Dunn.

"You?" says Dunn with a terrible contempt. He stands in the centre of the yard, hands on waist, glaring at the king. "I had my first billion before you was ever born!"

The king grips the rail. He's enraged by this insolence.

"You never had two bob in yer bloody life! It belongs ter me! I'm Throgmorton!"

"My arse!" sneers Dunn. "I knew Frogmorton six million years ago, before you was ever heard of!"

"I'm The Owner and The Maker!"

"You're bloody nothin'!"

Some of the men are beginning to take an interest. The Charge strolls from the office to listen and Fred Henderson and a couple of screws lay their cards down and turn in their chairs. Dunn is yelling that he could buy and sell Frogmorton a trillion times over.

"He's right, Silas," the Charge says.

"You're sacked!" barks the king.

"Aw Jeez, Silas, don't be hard on me," pleads the Charge.

"I said you're sacked! Pack yer bag and git orf the place!"

"Bah!" Dunn sneers. "You couldn't sack a bloody dog! I've sacked more blokes than you've had hot dinners!"

They argue over who's sacked more. Dunn has sacked forty-seven zillion, so he wins.

"What about them goldmines?" Fred Henderson chips in.

"They're mine!"

"I own the lot! Nine grillion of 'em!"

"What about the sheep stations?"

"I've got 'em all!"

"Ahhh, don't give me the bloody shits! I bought 'em all up six hundred centuries ago!"

"You're a liar!"

It goes on all morning, with Fred Henderson and the screws helping. Two of the screws are discussing whether they could tape-record it and maybe sell the tape in the pub. They reckon they'd get fifty dollars.

Bimbo is squatting beside Fred Henderson's chair. He's a bit worried by all the shouting, specially from the king who is closest.

"Willee root me?" he asks Fred.

"Hah! He couldn't root a fly!" says Dunn. "I've rooted nine thousand zillion ..."

But it isn't a fair contest because Silas has been ill.

Time can drag at weekends, though if the days are fine it's not so bad and you can stay in the yard and watch whatever there is to watch. You've begun trying to write poems about some of the men. That's a sign that you are more settled now. You can only write when you feel fairly settled. There is a wolfish man who spends all his time lying on the grass with his penis out, masturbating. He does it slowly to a climax and starts again. He takes no notice of female nurses or patients who pass by: whatever pictures are in his mind must be more exciting, and it'd be interesting to know what they are—for the poem you're trying to write. It seems almost, from the way he rubs his sperm into the soil, that he's impregnating the earth. It's as if the grass and trees and flowers of the world only happen because of this; as if all life and beauty flowed from him, the seed-giver. But everyone just calls him Wanker.

The wards alongside are familiar now. The wheelchairs in 7 stay parked on the lawn most of the time when it's fine, the figures in them slumped and the strings of spit dangling from the mouths. Occasionally one has a fit, arching and gurgling in the chair, and a nurse comes to deal with it while some of the retards gallop around like monkeys when there is a disturbance in a cage.

There are disturbances sometimes among the old women on the other side. You hear screams and long shrill arguments, and the voices of particular nurses who seem to control the women by outscreaming them. Mostly, though, it is quiet. The women are showered each Saturday in the shower room at the end of their verandah. From the bottom of REFRACT's yard you can see them milling naked at the door, waiting turns, being herded in. The first time you saw them you watched for a minute, slightly aroused by the shock of the nakedness. But they looked too helpless and broken. You felt you were gloating over the final sadness of their lives.

Outsiders often drive along the dirt road at weekends. They drive slowly and peer into the yards and laugh and point out the sights to one another.

"Struth, look at that one pullin' himself!"

"Hey, wanker!"

"You'll go mad doin' that!"

Or they'll just lean from their cars and call "Hey!" at you, as if you probably don't understand normal speech but might respond to a call and turn your head. There is a bunch of young toughs inching past in a panel van.

"Hey, want a peanut?" one of them calls to you.

"Don't you need it to think with?" you reply.

"Better not get fuckin' smart! I'll punch yer head in!"

"Be my guest," you say. "I'm afraid I can't come out so you'll have to come in."

You can hear the tough's mates egging him on.

"Flatten 'im, Terry!"

"Yeah, Terry, git over the fence an' wallop the cunt!"

Terry gazes into the yard, at the men. Especially at the huge hunchback who is huffing and beating his chest in what looks like bestial rage.

"Nah," says Terry the Tough to his pals. "I wouldn't waste me fuckin' time."

The panel van roars off, spinning its wheels.

The hunchback's name is Lloyd something. You don't know his surname and can't imagine him ever needing one. He's just Lloyd. He is usually very quiet and keeps to himself, grinning and muttering in a corner, twisting his big raw hands together, rubbing his big raw tongue over his chapped lips. If you go too close he'll give a little snuffle of embarrassment and shuffle away. If Terry the Tough had climbed the fence poor Lloyd would have retreated at once. Lloyd works in the hospital laundry, carrying fouled linen, and blokes say that he eats bits of shit he finds there. When he has his fits of agitation he runs about grunting and beating himself with his fists and tearing up clumps of grass and throwing them in the air. The screws tell him to stop the bloody nonsense and sometimes he does. Other times they threaten him with a needle. Lloyd looks somehow relieved when screws hold him down and jab the needle in. His ugly face softens, his breathing becomes regular, he sleeps. You think Lloyd has a love-hate relationship with the needle: he fears being held and jabbed, but wants the oblivion.

REFRACT holds mostly dills at the weekend. Blokes who aren't dills usually have parole to wander in the grounds. There are two kinds of parole—company and individual. Company parole lets you go around with another patient and the idea is that each keeps tabs on the other. Individual parole is harder to get. The only special rule for that is that you keep away from certain areas, like the staff cottages where doctors and their families live, some of the female wards, and particularly the Admission wards at the top end of the hospital. They don't like bottom-end riffraff near Admission. Fred Henderson calls Admission patients Silk Hankies.

"Pampered little cunts, stretched on couches, telling the quack about their bad dreams, havin' their foreheads wiped with silk hankies! They like to think they're in some nice sanitarium for 'nerves'. The sight of us scares the shit out of 'em!"

You wonder if you'll ever get parole. They'd be wary of giving it to a MAX man. Fred has it of course, but he's in with the screws. Dennis Lane had it, but look what happened to him. If you had parole you could walk along the dirt road and find where it goes when it curves past the library and the morgue. It must lead to the lake at that end. It'd be so good to walk to the lake and sit and look across. And it would seem odd to be that close to it. For nearly five years you watched the lake from the verandah of MAX, seeing it over the wall lower down on the slope. You learned the lake's colours and moods—the early morning sheet of sunlight that hurt your eyes, the midday blue with ruffles of white foam, the dark evening pool with the image of the moon or the first stars in it. Or you knew the lake as a foggy blur under sleet, the place where the wind got its run-up to whoosh along the verandah and whine in the barbed wire. Your lake is someone else's now. Someone in MAX is learning the colours and moods the way you did.

If you ever got parole it'd be company parole and there isn't anyone you'd want to go around with, no-one you could count on not to get you into trouble. Individual parole would suit you. You'd keep away from the forbidden areas and especially the Admission wards. You wouldn't want to interfere with anyone's illusions.

OT is better now you've got over being afraid of the old sewing machine. The main thing is to learn the right pressure to put on the treadle and so control the speed of the needle. If the needle isn't going too fast the thread won't tangle so often. The first few vinyl bags you made had to be cut apart and thrown in the scrap-bin. The seams came open, or you'd sewn panels in upside down. But then you did one pretty well and the process wasn't a mystery any more. Now you make half a dozen bags each day

Peter Kocan

and Mr Trowbridge is able to leave you to it. When Mr Trowbridge is sorting out the ten different problems on his mind he'll walk through the building pointing his long finger and ticking off what's okay: "Baskets okay. Painting okay. Vinyl bags okay..." The vinyl bag section gets ticked off most times now, which means you can feel fairly okay yourself. Each activity is called a section and you are the only person who is a section all by himself. You've never been a whole section before. Mr Trowbridge feels deeply that work is the best therapy for sick minds and he has a set of phrases about it. One is WORK MAKES WELL. The others aren't as catchy.

It's surprising how soon the bag work becomes boring. Now it is mid-afternoon and you have done your half-dozen bags and don't feel like beginning another. You'd like to sit looking out of the windows at the willows by the pond. The trees are catching the afternoon light. Or you'd like to turn your chair and just gaze at Cheryl, who is as beautiful as any tree with light on it. You feel a deep gratitude nowadays that you are allowed to be near women. Not just women. Cheryl. She's leaning over a table, helping someone plait a basket, and her long brown hair is back across her shoulder, slightly damp with sweat, and there are patches of sweat on the cloth of her uniform. She is hot and tired in the afternoon. A wave of love goes through you because she is tired and because she isn't as quick and clever as Janice and seldom wins the joking arguments they have. You and Cheryl don't speak much, but when you do she speaks like one person to another with only a trace of the nurse-to-patient tone; and even that trace is put on with an effort because she thinks it's the proper thing. But talking to Cheryl, or having her notice you, isn't so important. The great thing is being in the same room with her for six hours a day. Of course she isn't in the room all the time. She goes in and out, and it hurts when she isn't there.

You begin doodling a new bag design on a scrap of paper. You do this a lot now. Since you are the entire bag section you suppose new bag design comes within your jurisdiction. This one looks good—a ladies' shoulder-bag, small and neat with an outside pocket and adjustable strap. It should be two-tone in

110

colour and fastened with a little fancy turn-lock. You begin making a prototype. You can only work on it for a while each afternoon after your quota's done. You show it to Janice and Cheryl.

"Oooooh, it's *beautiful!*" cries Janice. She has an exaggerated way of speaking to patients, half-serious, half-mocking, the way a grown-up talks to a child. If you're a dill you respond to the serious part and if not you respond to the mocking and join in the game, like two adults discussing Santa Claus or something. But Janice will occasionally stop the game suddenly and leave you stranded, as though abruptly showing that she knows Santa isn't real and making it seem as though you don't.

"It's very nice, Len," Cheryl says simply.

"Get your eyes off it!" Janice tells her. "It's for me!"

They have a joking argument over it. Mr Trowbridge comes and they show it to him. He examines it and tells you it's an excellent piece of work. He's pleased, not with the bag as such but that you've shown initiative. The excitement dies very quickly and you don't bother making any more of the new style. It served its purpose. It let the staff see that you can turn your mind to things in a rational way.

Your stocks are raised also by the doctor's attitude. Electric Ned comes to OT one day. He's the doctor for REFRACT as well as MAX. He got his nickname because he likes giving shock treatment. He brings you a magazine with an article he thinks you may enjoy, something about culture.

"The part about the bush balladists is informative," he says.

"Mmmmm," you reply. "I'll read it with pleasure."

"Have you seen Len's new bag design?" Mr Trowbridge asks the doctor. He shows him the prototype and Electric Ned examines it through his thick lenses. Electric Ned is gratified. This tends to prove he was right to recommend you for OT. Mr Trowbridge is gratified. This indicates how much you are being helped at OT. You are pleased as well. You never get on better with staff than when they are taking credit for you.

All you think about now is Cheryl. Each evening when you return to REFRACT you go to the shower room and pull yourself. The shower room's the only private place in REFRACT. It's a large, cold room with cubicles and you can be alone there most times because the men don't shower much except on Saturday morning when the screws herd them in and stand ticking the names off a list as they come out drying themselves. You are in a cubicle, naked, pulling yourself madly and thinking about Cheryl, her beautiful legs in dark stockings, the way she looks when she bends across a table and her uniform rides up round her thighs. You get a crazy urge to run to OT right now, nude, with your prick out stiff and rub it against her. You get a picture of how funny it would look, and giggle hysterically. Then you feel desperate again and pull yourself harder and groan. A shriek comes from the next cubicle and you almost fall over with fright. Your heart thumps and your prick is suddenly limp and small in your hand.

"Who's there?" you ask in a tiny voice.

No answer. You don't know whether to look or not. It could be anyone. A screw even. It could be half a dozen blokes crouched in there for a lark, ready to leap out. You'll have to look.

You put your head round, ready to play innocent and ask for the soap or something. It's a man named Hogben. He's fighting his invisible enemy again. He has him in a headlock, pressed in a corner. Hogben's eyes are bulging and staring with the effort and his muscles taut with strain. Hogben's always cornering the invisible bloke like this.

"How ya goin'?" you say out of sheer relief that it's only Hogben.

He suddenly releases the headlock and lets go a flurry of uppercuts at the invisible bloke's belly. The invisible bloke seems to duck past and out of the shower room and Hogben goes after him. Hogben didn't even see you. He only saw the invisible bloke.

Of course you understand that your feelings about Cheryl are becoming a bit strong and could be dangerous for you. You understand that very clearly when you aren't near her, or thinking about her, or pulling yourself over her. The trouble is you are doing those things most of the time. At other moments you remember how Dennis Lane went stupid for his little retard bitch and what it cost him. Going stupid for a nurse could be fatal. Even the tiniest incident could destroy you. There are screws who'd be glad to pin something on you, something sexual and dirty like molesting a nurse, and by the time they finished blowing it up it'd sound as though you'd half-murdered her.

It is late afternoon and OT is almost deserted. You and Cheryl are alone in the room. It is very quiet. You are pretending to fiddle with a vinyl bag but you are really concentrating so hard on Cheryl that you can almost hear her breathing at the far end of the room.

"Will you help me with this, Len?" she says. She's putting finishing touches on a linen basket. She wants you to hold the satin lining in place inside the lid while she pins it. The job is awkward: you have to stand very close and she has to link her arms around yours and pin the satin between your spread fingers. Her fingers touch yours, and each time she leans to press a pin her head comes so close beside yours that you could kiss her ear. There's even a tiny pressure of her breast against your elbow. At least you think it's her breast. You don't dare take your eyes off the spot where the pin has to go. You're trying to keep all your senses open to take in every bit of this closeness so you'll remember what it was like. This is the most intimacy you've ever had with a girl. It may be the most you'll ever have.

Suddenly you feel overwhelmed. How kind she is! How sweet to give you this intimacy! All the loneliness of your life wells up in you. You want to put your arms around her and bury your face in her brown hair and let her sweet kindness wash over you. You almost do it and the face of Dennis Lane flashes in your mind and then vanishes and you begin to do it for real this time because you know Cheryl is all kindness and sweet pity and wouldn't report you or let you get in trouble. There's a crash as the linen box overbalances on to the floor. Cheryl jumps away. With elaborate calmness you bend to pick up the box and a cane-knife that fell with it, then as you straighten you see Cheryl's eyes flick to the knife and to your face and to the knife again. You lay the knife on the table. Carefully.

"It's my knock-off time," you say. You feel empty.

"Alright," she says softly, almost apologetically.

You go out the door.

"Len!" she calls.

"Yes?"

"Thanks for helping me."

"Any time," you say.

You walk back to the ward in a cool wind. You loved Cheryl once, but already it seems long ago.

4

"Hey, Acker!"

You are lying on the grass in the yard on Sunday when you hear the screw yell. He's a thickset young screw, a rugby player, and calls all inmates Acker, which he says is short for Acker Shitsburg. That's his joke. It isn't much of a joke but it's the only one he has.

"Hey, Acker!" he calls again. You and another bloke look up. "Not you, Acker!" he says, waving the other bloke off. "*You*, Acker!" You go up and the screw tells you there's a visitor. He seems a bit edgy about it. You go into the visiting room and the screw follows. A tall and sort of languid man rises and comes forward. It's the poet you used to exchange letters with. You've not met him before.

"Geoffrey Hawsley," he says. He's holding your hand in both of his and smiling at you from a height. He has on a fluffy blouse with puffed-out sleeves and a wide bandanna round his neck. He looks just like an artist, especially with his long hair all untidy.

"You a poof?" the screw asks him.

"My sexual taste is between myself and my paramours, of whichever gender," says Geoffrey Hawsley. "And, though I have been known to embrace the macabre, I can offer *you* no prospect of ever sharing my couch of joy."

The screw turns to you. "D'you know this creep?"

"Oh yes," you explain. "Geoffrey's a poet."

"A poet, eh?" The screw spits the word out.

"I sense that we are brother artists," says Geoffrey Hawsley, laying a slender finger on the screw's sleeve. "Some day you must show me your cave paintings."

"What?" says the screw, stepping away. He isn't sure whether to punch Geoffrey Hawsley or not.

"Don't apologise. We know how busy you must be. We shall endure your absence as the stoics of old."

"Fuckin' smartarse!" says the screw, moving to the door. "Just don't stay too long. We don't like queers hangin' round the place."

"Ah, crossness can be charming in some people. What a pity you aren't one of them."

The door slams.

"Thank goodness he's gone," says Geoffrey Hawsley. "It was such an effort being pleasant to him."

He takes your hand in his again. "So you're Len. Of course a meeting in the flesh—if you'll pardon the phrase—is almost superfluous. I have known your soul through your letters and poems. As you, I hope, have known mine."

"Yes," you say.

Geoffrey Hawsley sits and draws you down beside him.

"How often I've sat at the piano in twilight, playing some sad gossamer piece of Chopin's, your latest letter open before me, your newest poem on my lips."

"That's good," you say.

"You are one of the rare spirits."

"Oh, I dunno."

"How I have longed to visit you here in your bleak prison like poor Oscar in Reading Gaol. You too, Len, are composing from the depths your own great *De Profundis*." Geoffrey Hawsley clasps your hand tighter. "But we shall free you somehow! Then I shall take you among my friends. They're all talented, vivacious people. They'll adore you!"

It does give you a tingle of excitement. You imagine smoky little cafés, artistic chaps with beards, sensitive girls who do pottery and believe in free love. Maybe you could make friends with painters who have nude models in their studios.

"You are reading Balzac of course?"

"No."

"But my dear, you must!"

"Oh, I mainly read Owen and those."

"A mere phase. You'll grow out of it."

"I don't think so," you say. Geoffrey Hawsley catches your tone.

"I've offended you."

"Not much."

"Oh, I grant dear Wilfred's heart was in the right place, but he

116

and his ilk remained essentially Public-School philistines whining over their spoilt rugger match. Surely you see that?"

"I'm afraid I don't." You wish Geoffrey Hawsley would go.

"I could teach you so much. I could make you one of the rare spirits."

"I thought I was already."

Geoffrey Hawsley wags a finger at you. "You really ought not attempt sarcasm with one so much better at it than yourself, Len dear." He squeezes your hand. "But I forgive you, and shall spare no effort to unchain your bonds." He takes an odd little jar from his pocket. "For the moment, though, I can offer you only— paradise!"

"What is it?" you ask, examining the white powder.

"Heaven or hell, as you wish. I am acquainted with both."

You are suddenly very scared. And angry.

"Cocaine," whispers Geoffrey Hawsley, passing the open jar under your nose.

"Christ, put it away!"

"You're afraid?"

You're afraid alright. Not of the powdery stuff itself, but of its name. Whenever you've heard the name it's been connected with somebody dying, or getting twenty years. If the screws caught you now ...

The door opens and the Charge enters with the screw behind him. Geoffrey Hawsley has made the jar vanish and is smiling up at them.

"Ready to go?" asks the Charge.

"I can't tear myself away," Geoffrey Hawsley replies. "The decor is enchanting. Who's your decorator?"

"Visiting time's up."

"I'd considered this less a visit than a pilgrimage."

"You'd better go."

"But my dear chap, why?"

"I think you know what's in my mind."

"Anthropology isn't my subject."

"I have a duty to protect Len."

"Lucky Len!"

"Out!" snaps the Charge.

"Yeah, git!" the screw adds.

Yes, please go, you're thinking. And go carefully so as not to stumble and drop the jar. Geoffrey Hawsley rises and takes your hand.

"I fear I'm detaining these gentlemen. No doubt they wish to be off stoning a bear for their supper. Goodbye, my dear."

"Goodbye," you say, withdrawing your hand. "And I'd rather you didn't come again." You are saying that because you mean it. You don't want Geoffrey Hawsley or his jar anywhere near you. You are also saying it so the screws will know you've pissed him off.

"Et tu, Brute?" he says. "A pity. I might have made something of you. On second thoughts, probably not. Such unpromising material ..."

Geoffrey Hawsley goes out and the Charge goes behind to unlock for him. You hear keys jangle and then Geoffrey Hawsley thanking the Charge for his graciousness or something like that, then he's gone. It's uncomfortable for a few days, but the screws don't appear to blame you. They seem to think they've saved you from something. Moral ruin, you suppose.

You've got your own cell. You are supposed to call it a room. It's a nice cell, one of those along the side of the verandah, and you are between Fred Henderson and old Throgmorton. Throgmorton stays in most of the time, except when he dresses up in the blanket and tall hat with the toilet paper and goes to argue with Dunn across the yard. You hear Throgmorton at night, groaning that he's The Owner and The Maker and threatening to sack the staff. He's old and sick now, but in his prime he often sacked the Medical Superintendent, and once he sacked the Minister of Health who came on an inspection. You usually know when Fred Henderson's in his cell on the other side because Bimbo squats outside the door pointing to blokes in the yard and asking if they'll root him. "Fuckin' oath he will!" Fred yells back every so often to encourage Bimbo.

When you close the door the cell is fairly quiet and wonderfully private. There is a peephole and people can look in, but that's privacy compared to what you had. The bed is against the window and the window has heavy bars. You prefer barred windows. Outside is a stretch of dry dirt and scraggly grass and then the wall of Ward 7. Between the top of your window and the top of Ward 7's wall is a patch of sky. This dirt and grass and patch of sky belong to you. Not the things themselves but the angle of view. The blokes in other cells can see the same clump of weed or the same chimneypot on Ward 7's roof but from a slightly different angle. Your own precise angle is yours.

It's nice in the evening, sitting on the verandah outside your own door, watching the sky change. The setting sun lights the tiles of the roof opposite so that they glint like copper. A cool breeze comes up most evenings. The very best times are when hundreds of wild ducks fly over at sunset and you hear the whoosh of all the wings and the cries the ducks make.

They gave you this cell because you were next in line for one after Halliday was taken away with his bad head wound. It happened in the TV room one night. We were packed in there in the smoky haze and in the heat from the big old wood-burner they use in winter. Only a few blokes ever really watch TV. Most stay in the back of the room near the heater and the snooker table and the cards. You were in a chair near the TV, but you weren't watching the programme. You were studying Lloyd. Lloyd loves TV and has his own chair right in front. Everyone knows the chair is Lloyd's and they let him have it. A lot of places in the ward are like that. There's a vague sense that certain blokes sit or walk or lie in certain spots and so other blokes tend to go along with it. It isn't just politeness. The bottom left-hand corner of the yard, for instance, is where Hogben often traps his invisible bloke. If you were there when Hogben charges in with a flurry of punches he'd knock you black and blue without even noticing.

Lloyd enjoys ads. If a little cartoon man hops out of a washing machine to tell the amazed housewife about Wizzo detergent you'll see Lloyd squirm and giggle and twist his raw hands with glee. He likes jingles too, and any programme with beautiful girls. That night there was a nice ad that showed bikini girls on a beach drinking Coke. They were wet from the surf and the sun was making the drops glitter in a cascade whenever the girls tossed their hair back. They were very beautiful girls and Lloyd was staring and winding his hands and letting his big tongue loll the way he does when he's entranced.

"Whassat shit?" snorted an old dill from the back. The old dill normally sleeps curled in a chair halfway back in the room, except when he stirs to gob on the floor. Nobody takes any notice.

"Whassat fuckin' shit?" snorts the old dill again.

"Shuddup, ya stupid old mongrel!" says someone.

"Turn that fuckin' shit off!" the old dill croaks. He's out of his chair and stumbling forward.

"Drop dead, ya mad bastard!"

"I'll frigginwell break it!" the old dill yells.

"You couldn't break wind!"

"Can't I just?" mumbles the old dill. He staggers back to the wood box near the heater and picks up a lump of wood, then stumbles forward again, being kicked along the way, and waves the wood at the TV screen.

"I'll smash it!" he yells.

"Go on then!" It's Harris.

"Yeah, smash it!" urges someone else.

"Let's see yer do it!" cries Harris.

The old dill makes a violent motion to hurl the wood but brings it down hard on the back of a chair. It wouldn't have mattered except that Halliday's head was there. The screws come and look at Halliday who is unconscious and bleeding from the ears. One screw phones Electric Ned while the other drags the old dill to the isolation cell. Halliday is taken away on a stretcher and the screw details someone to mop up the blood.

They let the old dill out next day. The screws threaten him that when Halliday returns, if he returns, they'll look the other way for ten minutes. The old dill doesn't know what they're talking about. His mind's a blank.

But you've got a nice cell.

***

A movie is shown in the hall each Monday night and patients go or are taken from all over the hospital. REFRACT men who have parole can go by themselves and others who're interested are escorted by a screw. After three months you still haven't been. You love films and feel sick with envy seeing the group form up at the door each Monday after tea. You haven't asked to go. You'd assumed the Charge would tell you when he thought you were ready for the privilege. The same with parole. Other men, less well behaved than you, have it. It isn't fair. Being allowed to walk to and from OT unsupervised is a kind of parole perhaps, and you still feel amazed sometimes to be walking along by yourself without fences or wire or screws around you. But parole to walk in a straight line between two buildings isn't much, really. You worry when you find yourself thinking like this. Give Tarbutt an inch and he wants a mile!

It is Monday evening and the film group is gathering at the door where a screw is noting the names on a pad.

You go to the Charge.

"Excuse me. I was wondering if, um, er, I could . . ."

The Charge looks up from his newspaper. Already you regret this.

". . . go to the movie."

"Alright," he says and looks down again.

The screw adds your name to the list as if it's nothing at all. The screw unlocks and steps outside, then calls each man out and ticks his name. The names will be ticked again when we come back. There are eight of us. We walk along with the screw. The moon is enormous and there is a lovely soft breeze. This is the first time in years you've been out under a night sky. Our feet crunch on gravel past other wards and past dark clumps of trees. You keep your eyes wide open and take deep breaths, wanting to absorb it all. We are passing a ward—Ward 10 the sign says— and a young nurse comes out and calls to our screw. We stop while he goes to talk to her. They talk in low tones for a long time, but you don't care. You sit on a grassy bank all cool and bright under the big moon. The breeze is salty from the lake. Harris grumbles that we'll miss the movie.

"Listen, you Ackers," calls our screw. "I've got sumpthin' ter do. You go on by yerselves. I'll meet yous at the hall later."

We walk on.

"Dirty bugger!" says Harris. "I'll bet he's got sumpthin' ter do. I wouldn't mind doin' her meself."

"Hey!" the screw calls.

We stop.

"Any Acker pisses orf I'll have his guts fer garters!"

We go over a rise and there is the lake, a cool blaze of silver stretching away to a dark shore where dots of light wink. Car lights. A point juts from one side like a great black shadow on the ruffled silver.

The breeze is strong and salty.

"Whad'ya reckon about pissin' orf?" Harris asks the rest of us.

"Dunno," says another. "Whad'ya reckon?"

"Yeah, whad'ya reckon?" adds a third.

These are dills and what they do is no concern of yours, but you'd enjoy the joke of being the only one left to be ticked back into the ward.

"Nah, I'm not pissin' orf," says somebody.

"Me neither," adds another.

The consensus is for staying but Harris says he's had an arseful and walks into the darkness. We go on and are nearly at the hall. It is lit up and there are patients going inside and some screws round the entrance. Harris catches up with us.

"Aren't ya pissin' orf?"

"Nah," he says. "They reckon the movie ain't too bad."

A senior screw looks us over.

"Where yous from?"

"REFRACT," you tell him.

"Where's yer friggin' escort then?"

"Just back there," you say, pointing over your shoulder as though our screw is behind us.

The senior screw waves us inside. The hall is large and shabby, with rows of hard seats. There are more patients than you've seen in one place before. They are all kinds: little retards and old women, purple-faced epileptics, ones in wheelchairs parked in the aisles, ordinary dills in bunches, ones holding hands with their boyfriends and girlfriends. And there are six or seven who look almost normal. They sit slightly apart from the rest. They're young. Probably drug addicts or something. Admission ward types. Among them is a girl about sixteen with long plaits and a string of beads around her neck. You notice her because she has a quick nervous way of fiddling with the beads. Also because she's pretty. Hardly anyone in this hall is pretty.

The movie is a good one and you enjoy it, except that the screen is old and patched and the patches don't quite match. The projector keeps breaking down too and during the breaks the lights come on and the patients get even noisier than when the film is running.

Afterwards we find our screw outside. A retard girl is on the ground outside the door and won't get up. She is howling swearwords like a child who doesn't know what they mean but just knows they're nasty. She doesn't care that her nose is snotty and her dress hiked around her waist. When a nurse lifts her she kicks and howls and then chokes on the snot and coughs and throws herself down again. The crowd from the hall is trampling her arms and legs but she stays on the ground, screaming swearwords.

"It's hard ter credit, ain't it?" says our screw.

"What is?" you ask.

"That's what Dennis Lane did his knackers over."

5

Con Pappas has arrived from MAX. You didn't have much to do with him there. He was one of the hangdog ones in the background who never joined in jokes or sport. Besides, he was Greek and about forty-five. You wouldn't have tipped Con Pappas to get this transfer, but then a lot of people wouldn't have tipped you either. It's a lottery. Now he's here, though, you are glad to see him. Not having much in common doesn't matter. He was in MAX with you.

Con Pappas walks down the yard after his pep-talk from the Charge. He feels the way you did—lost and strange and nervous of the fence.

"Good on ya, mate!" you say. You shake hands.

"Good you too!" he says in his Greek accent.

"How are all the boys?" you ask. You really want to know. Also you need to show—show yourself mainly— that you are still with them in spirit.

"Ah, they are fifty-fifty," says Con Pappas with a hand gesture.

"How's Bill Greene?"

"Okay."

Okay is a sort of dead end. It means nothing's changed. You wonder what you expected.

"How's Ray Hoad?"

"He has trouble."

"What trouble?"

"Screws put lotta shit on him."

"How's he taking it?"

"He offer fight screw alone in cell. They will not. He offer fight two screws. They will not. He offer three. They will not."

No, you bet they won't. They know what's in Ray Hoad's mind. Some screws spout about not hiding behind the uniform and that they'll gladly box-on with any patient who fancies himself, but it's always rigged. It would only be a fair fight while the screw was winning. If he looked like losing it'd immediately

124

become an assault by a psychopath. The psychopath would get shock and the screws would demand extra danger money. Ray Hoad knows how rigged it would be but he wouldn't care as long as he got a few good punches in. Still, it probably isn't very smart of Ray Hoad to offer to fight screws, specially since Lubecki killed the Charge with that pitchfork.

You half-think to ask Con Pappas about Lubecki, but there isn't much point. Lubecki's finished. He'll die in MAX.

"Much trouble when Alan Bowers necked himself?" you ask. You heard about Alan Bowers a few weeks ago. Blokes sometimes hang themselves in MAX. It averages maybe one a year. There are forty or so men there normally so you could say the necking odds are forty to one. The transfer's a lottery and so is necking.

"No, not much trouble," says Con Pappas.

You wouldn't have expected much trouble. The necking is sort of rigged too. If you kill yourself it doesn't reflect on the staff too badly. It's just something you did to yourself. If you get on well, though, it's due to the staff's expert care. None of the credit is yours.

That subject is a dead end.

"How's Dennis Lane?" you ask.

Con Pappas looks uncomfortable. He saw Dennis Lane arrive back in MAX, so he knows transfers can be reversed.

"Very bad," says Con Pappas in a low voice. "Big medication. No can talk. No can walk. He is *kaput!*" Con Pappas stares at you. He wants to know what great danger is here.

"Why he sent back?"

"He was stupid."

"What kinda stupid?"

"Stupid with girl."

"Ah," whispers Con Pappas.

Fred Henderson comes down the yard with Bimbo. Fred wants to hear about the boys too. He has a good old wheeze over Dennis Lane being *kaput*. Bimbo's "Willee root me?" is irritating and when he starts showing Con Pappas the war dance you wander to your cell and sit thinking how all your questions about MAX led to dead ends.

Con Pappas is sent to OT and put in the vinyl bag section as your offsider. He cuts out the panels for you, and attaches the fittings. You concentrate on sewing. Mr Trowbridge wants as many bags as possible for the annual fete. Already you have five months' worth stacked in a pile.

After breakfast on the Sunday of the fete you stand at the bottom fence and watch the first cars nosing into the grounds. Banners have been strung and on the trees are signs with arrows pointing to where different attractions are to be, like speedboat races on the lake, or the hoop-las and merry-go-rounds, or the cake and drink stalls in the main hall. You can't see any of those, just the pointing arrows. The Charge says men without parole will be taken round after lunch to see the sights.

OT has a banner across the front: BASKETS + BAGS + WOODWORK FOR SALE. It's a good businesslike banner. But they've put another sign by the door, inviting the Public to Inspect this Facility and learn about Rehabilitation and Remotivation and other things with long names. You don't bother reading it properly. It's just for the Public.

By ten o'clock the crowds are beginning all along the dirt road and in and out of OT and back towards the main hall and the lake. You can hear speedboats. You watch to see if anyone is buying your bags and you begin to see more and more people emerging from OT with them. You get the impression that the vinyl bag section is pulling its weight today.

When the crowds get thicker you leave the fence and stay on the verandah near your cell. You can see the people from here without them seeing you. You don't mind them having the speedboats and hoop-las and cake stalls, but you don't intend to help them have the other thing they've come for—the freak show.

The people are mostly families with kids, or young couples holding hands. They are enjoying themselves. They stare into the yards from the dirt road. The wheelchair cases in Ward 7 are parked in a row across the grass, most with their heads sunk on their chests and the strings of bright spit hanging. They are supposed to be sharing the fun. The old women on the other side are wandering their yard sad and lost, like always. They have fresh dresses on. Not nice dresses, just washed ones. You wish they'd all be taken inside. They don't care about the freak show, or even know about it, but you wish they'd be taken inside.

Con Pappas is at the fence. This must be exciting for him. It's a bit exciting for you too. You sometimes think about going free and being in the ordinary world again, but you never imagined the ordinary world suddenly appearing here like this. You would like to be at the fence with Con Pappas where you could see the people close up and hear the talk and laughter, but not if it means giving them the other thing. Harris is at the fence.

A couple with a small girl stop and stare into the yard. Harris calls hello and asks for a cigarette. They nudge each other and giggle. Harris is pressing his purple epileptic face against the wire. "Garn, gis a fag!" he's saying. "Garn, gis a friggin' smoke, will ya!" The couple walk on but the small girl lags behind and comes skipping to the fence where Con Pappas is. Maybe she wants to show her green balloon. Con Pappas bends to speak to her through the wire. Greeks like children. You see Harris moving across.

"Rebecca!" screams the mother. "Come away quick!"

The father runs and yanks the girl away by the arm. Even from here you see the look he gives Con Pappas, a look that says animals like this ought to be put down or at least horsewhipped. "Gis a fuckin' smoke!" yells Harris. "Ya fuckin' tight-arsed cunt! Won't give a man a lousy fag!" Con Pappas comes up and sits near you. You're sorry it happened like that for him. Harris doesn't matter. All he knows is that he didn't get a fag.

But you are glad the couple had a fright about their little girl. Maybe they won't enjoy the rest of the freak show so much.

After lunch you stay in the cell and look at your patch of sky where some very high white clouds are floating. You watch the movement of them past the chimneypot on Ward 7. Already you are tired of speedboat noises and crowds from the ordinary world. If the screws take us around you'll go, but you don't care particularly.

Four people appear outside your window. Two spotty youths with their girlfriends. They are taking a short cut between the wards, and seeing what they can see.

"G'day," says the taller of the spotty youths.

"Hello," you say.

"You one of the loonies?"

"I'm a psychiatrist, actually."

"Yeah?" He half-believes you. You aren't screeching or tearing your hair.

"Listen, what're the maddies like?" he asks.

"You've not been an inmate yourself?"

"Course I bloody haven't!"

You are staring intently at his face.

"How long have you had that twitch?"

"What twitch?"

"Have you spoken to your own psychiatrist about it?"

"Haven't got a bloody psychiatrist!"

"Stay where you are. I'll come out. It's important I have a talk with you."

You go out of the cell and wait a moment. When you return to the window they have gone.

Harris's voice is loudly asking the screws when we'll be taken round. He's pestering them, making it sound as though they owe it to us because the Charge promised. He's forcing them to show they don't owe us anything, ever. All afternoon Harris keeps on until he's yelling that he'll make an Official Complaint. There's no such thing, but it's a mistake to threaten the screws with it. You hear them ordering Harris to shut his fucking snout before they shut it for him. Then you hear thuds and groans outside your cell. The thuds and groans happen there because it's shielded from the road. Noises like that always give you an awful churning in your stomach but this time it's almost worth it to have Harris's mouth shut.

Late in the afternoon Silas Throgmorton staggers out in his tall hat and blanket to argue with Dunn in the yard. Spectators gather on the dirt road, but Throgmorton is too sick and has to be helped inside before the quarrel warms up. The spectators drift away, unaware of what they've missed. They have also missed Lloyd. He's scared of crowds and has happily stayed watching TV all day. And Hogben's invisible bloke has kept him occupied in the shower room mostly. The Wanker has been locked in the dormitory. He's a bit much even for the freak show.

Harris is on his feet in time to farewell the last of the crowds as they diminish through the litter and half-light of evening.

"Garn, gis a fag ya dirty friggin' hoons!"

6

Men are going to walk on the moon this afternoon. The OT staff are urging everyone back to their wards to see the telecast. An old woman in the basket section doesn't want to.

"You have to," Cheryl tells her.

"Why?"

"People are going to walk on the moon."

"People can't do that."

"They can."

"They can't," insists the old woman. She's been here for forty-four years.

"I'm telling you they can," says Cheryl. As a nurse it's her job to put this poor creature into contact with reality.

"How would they get there?"

"In a spaceship."

"There's no such things as spaceships."

"Who told you that?"

"The doctor."

"When did he tell you?"

"Years and years ago."

"Well, there *are* spaceships."

"Why did the doctor say there weren't?"

"He didn't know about them."

"But I told him, and he said it wasn't true."

"That's right."

"You said he didn't know about them."

"He didn't."

"Was I right then?"

"No, because they didn't exist."

"Was the doctor right?"

"Yes."

"You said he didn't know about them."

"He didn't then, but he does now."

"He's dead."

"Well he'd know about them if he was alive."

"He was alive when he told me there weren't any."

"But he didn't know about them then."

"You said if he was alive he'd know."

"Look, *nobody* knew about them then."

"I did."

"You didn't. It wasn't true then. It's only true now."

"Is the Wires true now?" The Wires are something like electric powerlines across the universe. The old woman gets messages from the Wires.

"No, the Wires aren't true."

"Will they be true one day?"

"No, they're impossible."

"Like spaceships?"

"Spaceships *are* possible! You can see one on television this afterbloodynoon!"

"Was the doctor wrong?"

"Do you want a kick in the arse?"

"No."

"Then get back to your ward and watch bloody television!"

The old woman shuffles off, forty-four years of psychiatric treatment crumbling from her.

You and Cheryl and Janice go to Ward 7 to see the telecast.

"Gosh," says Cheryl. "How do they send pictures all that distance?"

"Along the Wires, of course," you say.

She punches you hard.

You're beginning to like Cheryl again.

The parole thing has been bothering you. Nobody's mentioned it. Con Pappas has got company parole already. You don't grudge him, but it seems a bit unfair. All you've got is the right to walk to OT and back, and the Monday night films. You can't even change a book at the library without a screw along and it's often hard to find a screw who'll take you. They call little escort jobs like that "extra work" and they say it'll break down their conditions if they do it too much.

You are fairly rich now. Mr Trowbridge has raised your pay to three dollars a week because the vinyl bags went so well at the fete. If you had parole you could hang about at the canteen and drink milkshakes and stuff. You suppose you must be getting soft. What would David Allison think of you? Milkshakes!

You wait till a day when the Charge seems in a good mood. You approach him outside the office.

"I wanted to ask about parole," you say.

"What about it?"

"Um, whether it'd be worthwhile applying for it." You don't just ask for it straight out. You aren't asking for it, but just broaching the subject, so if the answer is no it won't be a blunt refusal. It's always better to avoid blunt refusals.

The Charge looks at you sourly. You must have mistaken his mood.

"I think the doctor has other plans for you."

Your blood goes cold. Christ, what does "other plans" mean? In MAX the doctor's plans for people were mainly electrical. You try to think what you've done wrong. That's silly. There's no need for you to know what you've done wrong. You're just the patient.

"What does he have in mind?" you ask. Your voice is faint.

"He'll tell you," says the Charge as he turns his back and goes into the office.

For a week you hug yourself with worry. You haven't spoken to Electric Ned for ages. You thought he was satisfied with you. It must be something the screws reported. Maybe you've been keeping too much to yourself. "Withdrawn", they call it. You almost ask Mr Trowbridge if he's heard anything, but that might make him think you're worried. Being worried is a bad sign. Besides, the report, whatever it was, might have come from the OT staff. The fact that you seemed to be doing well at OT means nothing. Trouble like this can come when you feel most secure, usually does, in fact. You've let yourself feel stupidly secure lately—thinking about milkshakes.

If it's shock treatment you won't be able to stand it. Other men get through it. Con Pappas had it in MAX. Women have it.

You should be able to face it like they do but you know you can't. You get wild ideas of pissing off. You spend more time with Con Pappas, to show them you aren't as withdrawn as they thought, and because that makes the loneliness of the worry a little less. Also, being around someone who's had shock is a sort of reassurance that you'll be able to handle it yourself. Your stomach is a tight knot.

Then you do what you should have done at first. You read passages of *The Survivor*, like the part where David Allison has to go into action the first time. He is hugging a big old tree at the edge of a forest where the Prussian Guards are. In a moment he must take his rifle and join the line of his platoon and walk into the forest. He is hugging the tree and begging it to draw him inside itself and save him. He's remembering the time he stole another boy scout's compass and let someone else get the blame and now God is going to punish him and he's crying against the bark of the tree as though it's his mother's apron. Then a great kindness and calmness seem to come from the tree and unwrap his arms and push him gently forward. He walks into the forest with the others and the Prussian Guards charge at them and there is blood and screaming and he holds his bayonet up the way he was taught and suddenly it's over and he is a soldier who has fought the Prussian Guards and come out alive.

David Allison is with you. He's always with you, it's just that you forget sometimes. You feel ashamed. You aren't facing the Prussian Guards, just a fucking half-arsed quack with a two-dollar machine. Scared of shock? That'll be the day!

Electric Ned is coming along the verandah to your cell. You stay sitting on the bed, watching a grass stem bend in the breeze outside your window. Being in your cell like this is of course proof that you are withdrawn. Electric Ned is at the door.

"Mr Tarbutt."

"Yes," you say quietly.

Electric Ned enters. You don't bother rising.

"How are things?" He's staring through his thick lenses.

"About average."

"Feeling fine within yourself?"

"More or less."

"As you know, I've been following your progress in this ward and at OT. How do you think you've managed?"

"Reasonably," you say.

"Well, I think we need to do a bit more for you."

Yes, that'd be shock treatment. Shock is something they do "for you".

"I'm afraid the Medical Superintendent can't see his way to endorsing my proposal, so I've written to the Director-General seeking the go-ahead."

This is odd. Very odd.

"I propose to transfer you to an open ward."

A lot of screws don't like it. There is talk of a stop-work meeting. Letting criminal patients out of MAX into REFRACT is bad enough, but at least in REFRACT a criminal patient has some wire around him and still looks like a prisoner. It isn't personal, it's the principle. If you go to an open ward the flood-gates will burst and in six months there won't be a criminal patient left under lock and key.

The screws don't say much to you, just the odd remark, like when the Charge comes to your cell about some matter and looks around as if he's seeing the cell for the first time and says: "I'm sorry the accommodation is so humble, but I s'pose the doctor's out booking a hotel suite for you." Others refer to you as the Star Boarder.

You don't say anything. The transfer probably won't happen. It might be better if it doesn't. Being on the wrong side of the screws isn't worth it and if they want to make things hard for you it won't matter whether it's personal or for a principle. You can't understand why Electric Ned is doing this. Maybe he's gone crackers. That'd be a joke.

The transfer is approved after three weeks. Electric Ned is with you in the yard.

"Ward 24 has agreed to take you," he says.

"That's good," you say. You've no idea.

"Ward 24 has just been renovated, so you'll have pleasant surroundings at least."

"Sounds fine," you say, wondering about that "at least".

"Well," he says. "This marks the end of my responsibility for you. Ward 24 is under another doctor."

"I see," you reply. You hadn't thought of this. Electric Ned is the devil you know.

"Good luck." He offers his hand.

"Thanks for all you've done," you say.

"Oh, it's been a pleasure," he says and walks away.

He's your benefactor. You only wish he'd made that plain about five years ago. It would have saved you an awful lot of worry and anguish.

You sit for a while looking at the men and the fence and the dirt road and everything. Already they are beginning to seem different, the way things seem different when you know you'll never be at this exact relation to them again. The relation is of time, not space. Even if you make a cock-up of the transfer and land back here in a week it won't be the same.

After lunch you collect your gear and put it in the screw's car for the two-minute drive.

"What's 24 like?" you ask the screw.

"Not like anythin' yet," he says. "They're just reopening it today."

"What kind of patients will it have?"

"Low types."

"Why d'you say that?"

"Well, *you'll* be there, won't ya!"

7

It's high up, with a view of the lake and vast bushland. The view is better even than the one from MAX and you don't have to look at it through fences or across walls: there aren't any. You follow the screw across a wide courtyard and the Charge Sister meets us at the door. She's tall and bustling and wears a high starched veil. She's checking a clipboard with a list of names.

"Who's this?" she asks your screw.

"Lennie the Larrikin!" he says.

She gives him a look which says she's too busy to be mucked about, especially by a male.

"Tarbutt," the screw says.

She gives you a brisk glance and ticks the clipboard.

"Alright," she tells the screw. "You can go."

The screw turns away, giving you a thump on the arm and whispering, "Watch yourself, mate." He rolls his eyes back towards the Charge Sister and mutters, "Petticoat government!"

"You can put your things in the storeroom," the Charge Sister tells you. She sees another screw herding four or five other new arrivals and bustles off to them. They are retards, shuffling and squealing and dribbling.

You find the storeroom and leave your gear, then wander along a corridor to a huge dayroom. The whole building stinks of newness—paint, lino, vinyl, fabric. The dayroom is like a palace, or maybe an airport lounge, and spotless except for a long fresh smear of shit across the floor. The smear leads to a savage-looking bloke with wild hair sprawled in one of the new armchairs and stubbing a fag on it. There are a few others there. One of them's the retard girl that Dennis Lane went stupid for. She is sitting quietly staring with eyes very blue and wide open. Her hair is combed and she has a clean dress on. She looks rather sweet.

A young female nurse comes behind you and takes your sleeve between thumb and finger and asks—with deliberate clearness, so you'll understand—whether you've been allocated a bed yet. She seems surprised when you answer in a normal sort of way. She lets go your sleeve and leads you upstairs to a dormitory. It too is a blaze of newness. Bright orange bedspreads and curtains.

The nurse asks your name and you tell her and she points to a bed in the middle of a row.

"Is that end bed taken?" you ask.

She consults the bed plan she's holding. "No."

"Could I have it?"

"I've already marked you on the bed plan."

"Any chance of changing it?"

"I haven't got a rubber."

"Could you perhaps just cross it out?"

She's thinking about it. She's quite nice, really, but probably hasn't met a patient who cares which bed he has. She decides she can cross the name out.

"It'll look a bit messy, that's all."

"Sorry."

"Maybe I can find a rubber downstairs and fix it."

"Yes, I'm sorry."

She goes away and you sit on your new bed. It's right by the window and outside is a leafy branch and the wonderful view of the lake. You have the end bed, the window, the branch and the view. Men have killed for less.

The nurse comes back.

"I forgot. You aren't allowed in here except at bedtime."

Downstairs you find the ward is filling up. The corridors are crowded with patients, mostly retards by the look of them, and the screws and nurses who have brought them from all over the hospital. The Charge Sister is bustling with her clipboard and her own nurses are running about, following orders. Petticoat government seems efficient, at least. Most male screws treat nursing as a bit of a joke, unless "security" is involved. You suppose that's because protecting society from maniacs has some masculine style about it. Wiping bums hasn't much style.

You go outside and gaze at the lake. Then you move to the side of the building and look across the vast bushland. You can see MAX. It is small and far away, just red roofs and the red wall snaking around the ridge top and a glint of sun on the swimming pool. If you squint hard you can almost see men in the yard, but maybe you only think you see them. It is hard to believe you are here like this, seeing MAX so tiny. Those men who walked on the moon must have felt this way, looking back at the little earth.

It's two-thirty. You wonder if you are supposed to go to OT this afternoon. You want to. All this has unsettled you and you'd like to counteract it with a spell in your familiar corner at work. You find the Charge Sister in a throng of people and get her attention for a moment. Yes, you may go to work. You assume she means by yourself, but you aren't sure. Before you can clarify it she has turned away and you don't dare bother her again. You spend half an hour trying to figure if she meant by yourself or not. If you don't hurry up it won't be worth going. With a sense of taking a great risk you set off.

The walk takes five minutes, down a steep hill, past the Administration block—which makes you very nervous—and then down between Ward 7 and REFRACT. You pass the window of your own cell in REFRACT and you see that someone else has it already. At the next window you see Throgmorton's sick old face peering from the pillow.

"I'm The Owner and The Maker!" he croaks at you.

The little bandy-legged bloke hails you from the yard as you pass.

"Gettin' out Tuesday!"

It makes you homesick.

You've just sat down at your sewing machine and are telling Con Pappas about Ward 24 when Cheryl and Janice come from the office with a cake on a tray. It has green icing and a spiral of whipped cream on top. They set it down on the sewing machine and stand back grinning.

"What's this?" you ask.

"Your coming-out cake, of course!" says Janice.

"To celebrate going to an open ward," says Cheryl.

"Cheryl baked it," adds Janice. "So it'll probably kill you!"

***

The dining room is low and gloomy despite the fresh paint and the flashing stainless steel of the servery and the sinks and dishwashers behind it. Sixty patients are locked in here for the evening meal. The stink of us almost covers the reek of newness. They aren't all retards exactly. A lot are just chronics scraped from the back wards after twenty or so years. The ratio of sexes is about two-thirds male, one-third female. Many of them are still unsettled and they keep darting from their places and screws and nurses keep shoving them back in chairs. Already at this meal a table has been overturned and rissoles and gravy trodden to a mash on the floor. The rissoles are nice. You've eaten your first and are ready for the second when a bony hand snatches it. A screw grabs the wrist and bends it to make the hand let go. The rissole plops back into the plate and you get a splash of gravy. You don't feel like eating it now.

Most of these patients have name tags pinned on. The three men at your table are Stark, Stern and Gilroy—like a legal firm, or a comedy act. Stark is a thin dark retard. Stern is craggy-faced and addresses all staff as "Mr Attendant Sir". You don't see much of Gilroy. He keeps running around the room and screws keep shoving him down in the nearest chair. Now he's back—by accident, you think—in his own place.

The dining room has two doors. One leads on to the verandah and the other to the main corridor. Both lead to a version of The Gauntlet. After breakfast and lunch we are let out to the verandah where a file of screws and nurses waits to grab the worst of us and shove us into the lavatories to shit. After the evening meal we go into the corridor and another file waits at the stairs to shove the worst of us up to bed. The ones who aren't grabbed go through into the dayroom until ten o'clock. You could bear the stink and disruption of the dining room. The worst thing is wondering whether you'll get through The Gauntlet each time. You have only been grabbed once, so far. A young screw took hold of your collar at the stairs and began manhandling you up. The Charge Sister happened to notice and motioned him to let you go. You couldn't say anything. The indignity of it took your breath away.

You are in the dayroom tonight, in a kind of alcove which is designed to hold a billiard table or something. Of course there'd be no point having a billiard table in this ward. Billiards is too complicated for the likes of us. You are sitting alone, trying to read *The Survivor*. You're finding it hard to concentrate on anything any more except keeping yourself safe, and apart.

Deirdre sits near you. She's one of the four or five in this ward who seem fairly okay. She's about twenty-five, and works in the laundry. She worked at OT once but tried to break Mr Trowbridge's skull with a mallet so he got rid of her. There is an argument in the dayroom. A girl named Robyn is getting in trouble again. Robyn has cropped hair and a muscular body. Not ugly, just mannish. You think Robyn is fairly okay too, though she keeps painfully to herself and won't speak unless it's to argue with the staff in a sullen way. Robyn reminds you of yourself a few years ago when you were free. She's a "schizoid" type too. She thinks it's just her against the whole world. Of course, she's right.

"Robyn's bellyaching again," says Deirdre.

"She looks like a boy, doesn't she?" you say, just to make conversation.

"I wish she was," Deirdre says, giving you a look. "She's in the bed next to mine."

You sit thinking about that. Deirdre stretches, pushing her chest out.

"God, I feel like having sex!" she tells you. Then she asks, "Ever had sex?"

"Of course," you say.

"Want to have it now?"

"Aw, better not," you answer as casually as you can. Your heart is thumping. It'd be your first time. Maybe your only time ever. But you'd be crazy to get involved like that with Deirdre. And besides, you'd be scared of having it. You wouldn't know quite what to do.

Deirdre acts disappointed and wanders away. You sit trying to decide whether you've just had a lucky escape or a terrible loss. It seems both.

At ten o'clock we are put to bed. The dormitory smells very bad from the men who have been in there since six and there is a pool of piss on the floor at the foot of your bed. The night-screw

and his female nurse stand at the door watching while we undress.
You don't want to strip completely with the nurse watching so
you go to put your pyjamas on over your underpants.

"Hey, take off yer bloody undies!" the screw snaps. "You
don't sleep in yer bloody undies!"

So you take them off, hurriedly, in front of the nurse. There's
no point saying anything.

You sleep only in brief snatches. The light-switches are inside
the dormitory and some of the retards like to play with them. And
men keep coming to the foot of your bed to piss against the wall.
Stark even shits there. You hear him groaning and straining and
then a stink rises. You decide to clean it up, to take the smell
away, and because the screws might think it was you if they see it
near your bed. You get paper from the lavatory and then turn the
lights on so you can see what you're doing. You start cleaning the
shit up and someone turns the lights out. You turn them on again
and someone else puts them off. The next time you switch them
on somebody begins shouting abuse. It's the savage-looking bloke
who made the shit smear in the dayroom. He comes at you, his
face twisted with rage or madness or whatever it is that's wrong
with him. You don't want trouble. You tell him you only want the
lights for a moment, but he shapes to punch you, not because of
the lights—he doesn't care when the retards play with them—but
because you personally have some effect on him. His brute
stupidity suddenly seems too much to bear. You could belt him
senseless! Wipe his imbecile snarl right off! But you must avoid
trouble, so you turn the lights off and sneak back to your own end
to pick the shit up as best you can in the dark. Your fingers are
messy with it and your feet wet from the pool of piss. You go to
the showers and scrub yourself until your skin is sore.

You get used to blokes pissing around your bed. It's harder to
get used to the man in the next bed who sits up smoking all night
and tossing his butts across. You wonder whether these hard,
grey institutional blankets are prone to catch fire. By the morning
there are several small burn holes in them.

At six-thirty the Charge Sister and other screws and nurses
bustle in and haul everyone from bed and herd the worst retards

into the showers. They begin dressing some of the others and then remaking the beds. You jump up and dress quickly.

"Get in the shower!" a screw tells you.

"I had a shower during the night," you say.

"Get in the shower!"

So you take your towel and head towards the showers.

"Take yer bloody clothes off!" the screw snaps.

"I intend to," you say.

"Take 'em off now!"

So you return to your bed and undress and wrap the towel around yourself and go to the showers. There is a press of men in there and you wait naked and cold for your turn. When your turn comes you hang the towel on a rail outside the cubicle. When you reach for it it's gone. You dry yourself a bit with paper hand-towels, but you've nothing to wrap round yourself to go back through the dormitory where the female nurses are now busily making beds. You are cold and damp and your skin is itching from not being dried properly. The screw in charge of the showering sees you hanging about and tells you to piss off. A retard drops his towel beside you and you grab it quick and hurry back to your clothes.

A young nurse is about to begin making your bed but she realises she's stepping in piss and backs off, making a face. The screw comes over.

"You been pissin' here?"

"No."

"No, it don't bloody look like it, does it!" he snarls. "Go get a mop and clean it up!"

So you go to find a mop, with just the towel around you, and another nurse tells you to get dressed quick and lively instead of fart-arsing about. You mop the piss and then dress and then make your own bed. You're the only one in the dormitory who is able to make his own bed.

You hurry downstairs and count the minutes till breakfast is over and The Gauntlet is run and you can escape to OT. Of course every night in Ward 24 isn't like this. Sometimes all that happens is that you get in trouble for smoking in bed and burning holes in your blankets.

8

When you aren't at OT you sit at a spot at the side of the ward where you can be alone with the view of the sky and lake and bushland stretching away to MAX tiny in the distance. Years ago you invented something called the Principle of the Outward View. It was just the idea that, to minimise the mental effect of being locked up, you had to minimise the physical sense of it, so you'd try to keep open vistas in sight as much as possible. The sky is the biggest vista, and in MAX there was always the lake. The Principle of the Outward View was all about positioning: you'd sit outside rather than inside, near a window rather than away from it. If you could *see* great free spaces you could project your mind *into* them. It seems odd that you've never needed the Principle of the Outward View as much as you do now—in a ward without walls or fences.

The problem with this private spot is that you can't hear the meals called, and a couple of times you've gone late into the dining room and been told by the Charge Sister that you'll have to smarten yourself up. So now when you know mealtime is getting close you have to keep putting your head round the corner to check whether the other patients are still in the courtyard. The staff have noticed. It must look as if you are very anxious and irrational, bobbing back and forth around the corner like this. The staff have noticed a lot of things—like how you tried to take a shower with your clothes on and that you sleep in your undies and that you piss on the floor and burn your blankets and that you dry yourself with paper hand-towels. They are trained to notice significant details.

You've been here a couple of weeks. You are in your private spot at the side when a woman comes up a rough little path to the ward. She is middle-aged and sort of glamorous-looking. She's watching you closely as she approaches. You don't want to seem rude so you pretend not to notice her. She passes right by you and enters the ward. A minute later a nurse comes out.

"The doctor wants to see you," she says.

You go to the office and the woman is there. She asks you to sit down. She has a German accent.

"How are you feelink?"

"Alright, thanks."

She's watching you intently. Once or twice you meet her eyes but mostly you look at the floor.

"You are heppy to be here vis us?"

"Yes," you say. You can't tell her that this is the worst place you've been in in your whole life.

"And vot do you do vis yourself?"

"I work at OT."

"Ach, yes. Mr Trowbridge tells me you are good vorker. But vot else?"

"How do you mean?"

"You hev interests?"

"I read a fair bit."

"Ach, reading. And vot more?"

"I sit and think," you say, knowing immediately it's a mistake. The doctor narrows her eyes and purses her lips.

"Zat is not so healthy, eh?"

"I find it okay," you say. You must stick with it now or she'll get you for contradicting yourself.

"Vot do you tink about?"

"Oh, things I've read."

"Vot tinks you read?"

"Various books."

She indicates the book you have with you.

"Show me zat book."

You'd rather not. It's *The Survivor*. You don't want your holy book soiled by all this. You hand it over and she thumbs the pages. She's stolen your strength.

"Vot is about?"

"The Great War."

"Readink of vor is not so healthy, eh?"

"I suppose not," you reply. You are too depressed now to defend yourself. And too tired. You need to be fresh for dangerous occasions like this, but you've not slept properly for two weeks.

The doctor hands the book back and you go out, knowing how badly it went. Specially the confession that you think. Zat is not so healthy, eh?

Next morning you are leaving for OT and the Charge Sister stops you. "Doctor wants you at Group Therapy." This is something new. In MAX and REFRACT they didn't bother with stuff like Group Therapy.

We are in the dayroom, our chairs in a semicircle around the doctor's chair. All the worst retards and chronics are here, with nurses and screws to keep order. You are near the end of a row between Gilroy and Stern. The doctor is gazing at us. You think of her as "The German".

"How is everyone zis mornink?"

Two or three mumble replies. The question is too hard for the rest. You keep silent.

"Who knows vot day is today?"

Nobody responds.

"Is it Monday?" she prompts.

"Yes, Attendant Sir," says Stern.

"Who else tinks it is Monday?" asks "The German".

A few mumble agreement.

"Zat is wrong," she tells us. "It is maybe Tuesday?"

"Tuesday, Attendant Sir."

Again a murmur of agreement.

"Zat is wrong."

You realise the Group Therapy has begun. This is it.

"Who can guess vot day is today?" "The German" is gazing around the semicircle and now her eyes are on you. You can't believe this is happening. Does she think you belong here? That this is your level? You sit hunched within yourself, trying to show that you have enough self-respect to resent this. That's foolish. You aren't supposed to have self-respect. And your stomach is churning because you have already grasped how perfect this trap is. If you answer the question it will put you on a level with these others. If you don't answer it will put you on the level just the same.

"Vot does Len say?"

You try to look blank, as if you haven't been paying attention, as if you need to make an effort to descend to such nonsense. Of course the trap is too good. Disinterest and vagueness will show you are out of touch with reality and therefore belong in Group Therapy. Interest and acuteness will show you are being stimulated and therefore belong here just the same. You decide you'll have to answer.

"Thursday," you say, hoping to God it *is* Thursday. You try to put the exact edge on your voice to let her know that you understand the game, the trap, and are playing along out of contempt for it. But you mustn't really convey contempt. Contempt is a form of aggression and a symptom of paranoia and aggressive paranoiacs belong in Group Therapy. And you mustn't actually show that you understand the trap either. A patient who thinks the system is a set of traps has a persecution complex and belongs in Group Therapy.

And so you mutter "Thursday" and "The German" gives you a sort of verbal pat on the head, the way you'd do for a five-year-old who'd got a sum right, and the Group Therapy goes on to other subjects—like what the Big Bad Wolf said before he blew down the Piggies' house, or the name of the palace where the Queen lives. Whenever the others are stuck "The German" asks you and you have to answer.

We have Group Therapy twice a week.

Mr Trowbridge doesn't like you being kept from OT two mornings each week. "Bloody stupidity!" he says when you tell him about being the star five-year-old. His theory of Work seems wonderfully sensible now. If the patient can do his job he's alright, or fairly alright, and if he can't, he isn't. No traps in that. Mr Trowbridge isn't popular in the hospital. They say he's lost sight of psychiatric principles.

Cheryl and Janice sympathise. Sometimes when you get to OT after a Group Therapy session you make a joke of it.

"Do you know what Miss Muffet sat on?" you ask.

They think hard.

"A pin?" suggests Cheryl.

"The Three Bears' porridge?" offers Janice.

"Her tuffet!" you cry, clapping your hands in infant glee. They look astonished.

But you don't often feel like joking.

Con Pappas envies you being in an open ward. You try to tell him what it's like but he doesn't get your gist. Besides, you told him about Deirdre wanting sex and it's all he can think of.

You've begun walking in the hospital grounds. It's a bit awkward: you are allowed to go to and from OT and the Charge Sister lets you go to the Monday night films by yourself, but you don't know whether you actually have ground parole. In an open ward ground parole is probably automatic but being a criminal patient it may not be automatic for you. You don't ask. Better to play it by ear. You begin walking back from OT each evening by a longer route—along past the library and the morgue and then past the canteen and along the road by the lake shore, until you turn up the hill across an open stretch of paddock to the scrubby path which brings you to the ward courtyard. There are kangaroos lazing on the paddock sometimes. They are very tame and live by raiding rubbish bins outside various wards.

You walk briskly the first few times, to show you aren't loitering in places you've no business in. Gradually you relax your pace until you feel able to stop at the canteen for a few minutes each evening. You buy a milkshake most times. Girls serve behind the counter and you sit and watch them from the corner of your eye. Some of them are pretty. They're just ordinary girls from outside and you can listen to them talking to each other about outside things. Of course you mustn't act like a normal customer. You mustn't say anything if they give you the wrong change or if they ignore you when you are waiting to be served. If you said anything it would mean you were dangerously aggressive and ought not be loose. But you still like going there.

The evening walk is the best thing in your life now. When you come out of OT the noise and dust and the cooped-up feeling go out of you and you walk along feeling free as a bird, and when you go over the rise near the canteen the lake is suddenly spread in front of you and you feel the lovely rush of salty breeze. However bad you feel, that first sight of the lake perks you up and for a while you feel able to face anything. It isn't happiness, but just a sense of there being permanent and beautiful things in the world which will not be spoiled no matter what happens to yourself. Poetry is like that too. Every evening when you see the lake you get an urge to write again. But the urge is gone after five minutes back in the ward.

You have walks at weekends too. Not too conspicuously. You just wander to one or two special spots at the lake shore where you are screened from view and can read or simply stare at the sky and water and the line of green shore far away. The first couple of weekends, when you stayed in the ward the whole time, you got so desperate you decided you'd get away to your private spots even if they hanged you for it.

You can't make a stable relationship with the staff here the way you could in MAX or REFRACT. In those wards the screws tended to be the same ones most of the time, so they got to know you: not as a person, exactly, but at least as a name and a face and a pattern of behaviour. And being male screws they weren't interested in playing Florence Nightingale. You could come to a sort of understanding—the less trouble you caused them the more time they'd have to play cards or read the paper or listen to the races. In return they'd leave you alone in all sorts of small ways which were trivial in themselves but important to you. The understanding wasn't perfect. There were always a few screws throwing their weight about. The understanding worked in a general way. In this ward the atmosphere is always brisk and bustling and emotional. Florence Nightingale is big here. Not the saintly lady with the lamp but the organising busybody. The staff here don't know you. They chop and change. They have dozens of shitty bums and dribbling mouths to busybody with, and since bums and mouths are anonymous and interchangeable you're seen as a bum and mouth too. The screw who grabs your collar at the stairs might be male but the atmosphere that makes it happen is created by the Charge Sister and her petticoat government.

What really frightens you is that once the staff have made the assumption that you're a bum and mouth nothing you say seems to register.

It is the end of the midday meal and we are being herded out to the verandah for The Gauntlet. Mostly you slip through, but today a nurse grabs your arm and begins walking you to the lavatory. You can't pull away or throw her hand off—that'd be aggression—so you must let yourself be pulled along. The way a retard would.

"I'm afraid this is a mistake," you say as clearly and precisely as you can. "I'm quite able to arrange my own toilet habits."

But it doesn't register.

"Look," you say. "If you check with the Charge Sister I'm sure she'll confirm what I say."

But it doesn't register.

You take hold of the lavatory door as she tries to bundle you through. Passive resistance. Just like a retard. A screw sees you giving this nurse trouble and yells at you to get in the bloody dunny before he knocks your block off.

"Look, this is unnecessary!" you tell him. Your voice has gone trembly and you have an awful thought that maybe you only *think* you are speaking normally. You might be grunting like a retard and don't realise it.

The screw starts bending your arm up your back and the nurse walks off. Then a scuffle begins beside you and the screw turns to deal with it and you are able to slip away.

You don't want to exaggerate. You aren't treated as a retard all the time. Twice a week at Group Therapy you are promoted to a bright five-year-old.

9

The lake shore is often quite busy at weekends. Patients wander about, coming and going from the canteen, and sometimes there are people swimming or boating. Visitors have picnics on the grass with the patients they've come to see. You often find Stark there with his mother on Sunday. She's a quiet, elderly lady who brings sandwiches and cake and lemonade. She lays the stuff out on a cloth and they sit on either side of it. Stark is sometimes docile and sits chewing at the food and letting his mother wipe his mouth with a bib. Other times he'll spit and gurgle and toss the food away and kick the lemonade over. His mother's manner never changes. She talks to him quietly about the weather or something, as though it's really very pleasant to be having this picnic.

"What are those birds, Clifton?" she says when some pelicans fly overhead and settle on the water. "Pelicans I suppose. I don't know about birds much. You're lucky to have so many birds here, aren't you, Clifton? Had enough sandwiches? Do try some cake, dear. I'd hate it to go to waste. Gosh, isn't the sun warm now? Would you like your sunhat, Clifton? Yes, I think so ..."

When patients wander past and eye the food and lemonade Mrs Stark will treat them as friends of Clifton and invite them to share the picnic. She seems relieved when someone else is there. The conversation goes better. You and Con Pappas are going past and Clifton's mother calls hello and asks if we'd like to help finish up the sandwiches. You'd rather not. It's too sad. And you see enough of Clifton in the dining room. But Con Pappas wants to.

"It's nice to meet Clifton's friends," Mrs Stark tells us.

"Ah, Clifton is good man," says Con Pappas. He doesn't know Clifton from a bar of soap, but Greeks are polite.

"Which ward do you belong to?" asks Mrs Stark.

"REFRACT," says Con Pappas.

"Is it nice there?"

Con Pappas understands that it has to be nice. All the wards are nice. This is a nice institution.

"Is nice," he tells her. Maybe he really thinks so. He's awfully glad to be out of MAX and to have parole like this.

"You're from that ward too?" she asks you.

"I'm from Ward 24," you say.

"Oh, that's Clifton's ward. I didn't realise you and Clifton were such close friends."

"Yes, we're good mates," you say.

"Isn't that lovely!"

Mrs Stark gives us more cake and lemonade and we sit talking in the sun. She seems almost happy. A girl comes along the water's edge, walking a bit aimlessly and twisting some beads around her neck and stopping to stare at the lake. Mrs Stark calls to her about helping to finish off the food. The girl hesitates and twists the beads. Mrs Stark prompts the girl with the bit about the food only going to waste if it isn't finished up.

"Alright," the girl says. She sits cross-legged and accepts some cake and nibbles it. She keeps her eyes down, not from shyness but as though she's thinking her own thoughts. She doesn't seem shy.

"I suppose you all know each other," says Mrs Stark.

"No," says the girl, looking up briefly.

"Well," says Mrs Stark, "these are two of Clifton's friends."

We stay there, awkwardly, until Con Pappas says he must get back. His parole ends at twelve and begins again at two. You and the girl rise also. We all thank Mrs Stark for our nice time. Con Pappas goes. Mrs Stark is looking intently at you.

"Can I ask you a favour?" she says.

"Sure," you reply. She probably wants you to do an errand to the canteen.

"Look after Clifton. I mean, keep an eye on him if you can." She's a sad old woman.

You don't like to say that you've nothing to spare from looking after yourself and that Clifton would be better off dead, so you just nod and smile as though you appreciate the gravity of it.

You walk away and to your surprise the girl walks with you.

"What's wrong with Clifton?" she asks.

"He's a cabbage."

"She shouldn't have asked you that favour."

"It doesn't matter. It's just words."

"Won't you be able to look after him?"

"Oh, he's in his element in Ward 24. *He* should be looking after *me*."

"Ward 24 sounds awful."

"It is."

"So's Admission."

"I thought you were from Admission."

"Why?"

"You look the type."

"How does the type look?"

"More normal, less downtrodden."

"God! If you only knew!"

"A bloke I know calls Admission types the 'Silk Hankies'."

"Why?"

"He reckons you're all pampered."

"He should try it some time!"

The girl sounds offended. You don't want to offend her. It's lovely walking along like this, being able to talk so easily. You've never felt this comfortable with a girl. And she's nice-looking.

"I'm just telling you this other bloke's opinion. I wouldn't know, myself."

"Have you been here long?" She's lost the offended tone.

"Five and a half years."

"Jesus! What for?"

"It's a long story. What about you?"

"A fortnight, this time."

"I saw you at the Monday night film a couple of months ago."

"I've been home since then. Now I'm back."

"You were wearing those same beads."

"They're stupid, aren't they? Worry beads. I wear them to fiddle with."

"They're okay."

We are at Ward 24 now. You feel hollow at having to leave her.

"I have to go in," you say. "We get in trouble if we're late for meals."

"Alright," she says.

"Thanks for walking up with me."

"I was coming this way in any case," she says.

You feel as if she's slapped you. She didn't have to say that.

"Bye then," you say curtly, to show you don't give a stuff.

"Listen, would you like to have another walk after lunch?"

"If you like." A great relief is flooding you.

"I'll meet you at the canteen. Okay?"

"See you there."

You start up the scrubby path to the courtyard and she begins going along the road towards Admission.

"Hey!" she calls. "What's your name?"

"Len. What's yours?"

"Julie."

"I don't want to sound awful, but would you mind telling me why you're in this place?"

You are sitting with Julie at the lake shore.

"It isn't especially interesting."

"You don't have to. It's just that we're warned in Admission to be careful who we mix with."

"I'm not an axe-murderer."

"I didn't think you were."

"Are you?"

"Yes. Are you shocked?"

"Not at all. Some of my best friends are axe-murderers."

Julie stares at you.

"You're serious, aren't you?"

"Well, I have known a couple."

"How?"

"In MAX."

"What's that?"

You tell her about MAX.

"Why were you there? Please tell me. I'll feel scared if I don't know."

153

"You might be more scared if you do," you say, then regret it. She does look slightly scared. So you tell her what you did to get the Life sentence.

"Why did you do it?"

"To make a name for myself."

"Bullshit!"

"Well, it *was* more complicated than that, but that's how the media simplified it."

"I vaguely remember now. It was big news."

"They were wrapping fish and chips with it the next day."

"I'm glad you've told me. It's weird, but sort of *normal* weird. Not like being a maniac."

"I'm glad you think so. And what about your axe-murders?"

"Nothing so dramatic. It was just drugs. My family was hassling me so I went and lived with this guy for a while. I was only fifteen then. The cops got him."

"Carnal knowledge?"

"No, he was stripping cars more than he was stripping me. Anyway, my family arranged that I'd come here for treatment for the drugs. Mainly to save me from being declared 'in moral danger' or whatever they call it."

"Are you still a drug fiend?"

"Never was, really. It was pot mostly. I sniffed cocaine a few times but I didn't get wrapped in it. My family is very straight. They think anything stronger than a Bex and you're doomed."

We are leaning back on our elbows, watching little waves break at the edge of the grass near our feet. Julie's feet are small, but not dainty. They're strong and tanned in open sandals. You've always found feet vaguely embarrassing, but not Julie's. It's strange how easy it is to be with her. You read once that when you meet a girl you really like there aren't any lightning flashes or bells or great spasms of desire, just a relaxed warmth. That's how it is now. Julie is exciting and ordinary at the same time. Exciting because she's a girl and you can see her small firm breasts against her shirt, and ordinary because she's just a person and not a goddess or anything.

"How long will you be here this time?" you ask.

"Don't know. A few weeks I s'pose. I could sign myself out if I wanted but my family hassles me at home so I might as well be hassled here by professionals."

You don't know what to say to that. You've never met anyone who was here without having to be.

"What about you?"

"Life sentence," you say with a shrug. "I told you."

"What does that actually *mean*?"

"About seventeen years in this State."

Julie looks pained. You explain that you don't really know how long it'll be. Your position is complicated. Your crime was unusual and nobody knows exactly how much punishment it deserves. And you're doing your time here instead of in gaol, which complicates it more.

"Don't you ever think of escaping?"

"No."

"Don't you want to be free?"

"I'm only interested in being free in *here*," you say, tapping your head.

"And are you?"

"Not entirely, but I've no reason to think escaping would help."

Julie is gazing into your eyes. You gaze back. She has nice eyes and you don't mind them on you.

"You're supercool aren't you?" she says. "If they told me I might be here for seventeen years I'd die of fright."

"I have done many times."

"No you haven't. You're supercool. That was the first thing I sensed about you."

This is fascinating. You have spent years wondering how you appear to others.

"Supercool, eh?" you say, hoping she'll continue.

"Maybe that's the wrong word."

"What's the right word?"

"I don't know. It's as if nothing could ever surprise you. As though you know some big secret about life."

"I do."

"What is it?"

"Fatalism, basically."

"Which means?"

"That there's a bullet somewhere with your name on it. Or an accident, or a disease, or old age. Old age is the biggest bullet of all."

"Why d'you think that way?"

"I'm a spiritual member of the Lost Generation, living on borrowed time from Flanders."

You've never said it straightforwardly like that to anyone before. Julie at least half-understands. Wonderful girl! You tell her about *The Survivor* and David Allison and the poetry. As soon as you mention the poetry Julie recites some lines to you.

"Who's that by?"

"Emily Dickinson. I wrote a prize essay on her at school."

Astonishing girl!

It's getting late and turning chilly. We get up and walk along.

"Would you like to come round to Admission later? They have a rumpus room at the back. We could play records or something."

"I wouldn't be allowed," you say. You are wondering if you'll be grabbed at the stairs tonight. You can't bear the thought of it. Being with Julie has begun to give you back something. Perhaps the sense of being a real person. That's an awkward sense to have if you are very possibly going to be grabbed by the collar and kicked up some stairs.

"I'll come and see you then."

"You wouldn't like my ward. Anyway, they wouldn't let you in," you say. Then you add quickly, so she'll know you really want to keep seeing her: "Want to go to the film tomorrow night?"

"Okay."

"I'll meet you at the canteen at, say, six."

"Okay."

"By the way, how old are you?"

"Seventeen."

"I'm twenty-five."

"Poor old codger," she says, smiling.

***

There is an hour before the film starts so you and Julie have a walk along the lake shore. It seems natural to hold hands. When we go into the hall we see some young Admission patients and Julie leads you over and introduces you to one or two, then we sit at the end of their row, against the wall. We hold hands the whole time. Julie is clasping your hand between both of hers and letting it rest on her lap, then she rests her hand on your lap and it feels lovely when it makes a slight pressure where your prick is. The nicest thing is that it doesn't seem deliberate but just as if we are relaxed enough to touch like this without even thinking. You are thinking though—you're thinking how this is the first time you've held hands with a girl in the pictures. At twenty-five you are getting a taste of life!

Afterwards we stand in shadows outside your ward.

"What are you doing tomorrow?" she asks.

"I have to work at OT. What about you?"

"We have Group Therapy and stuff."

"Is it garbage?"

"Pretty much."

"I leave OT at four."

"Where's OT exactly? I'll meet you outside."

So it's arranged. You want to kiss her here in the shadows, but you aren't sure how to make the right movement so it'll seem natural. Julie makes the movement. Her mouth is very soft and when you feel her tongue against yours you go weak and hold her tighter, then step away slightly so she won't feel your prick getting hard. Half your mind is terribly clear and you are like a bystander watching yourself with this girl, as though you need a witness to tell you it's truly happening; the other half is like a gibbering idiot who wants to kiss her and fuck her and cry on her shoulder all at the same time.

Julie meets you the next evening and the two of you wander to a nice spot at the lake shore. You have your hand on the front of her blouse.

"I'm an idiot!" she says.

"Why?"

"Wearing this blouse with buttons on the back."

"You're a darling."

"I left my bra off but forgot about these buttons."

"It doesn't matter."

"You can undo it at the back if you want."

"I'd like to, but someone might come along. I don't want anyone seeing you half-undressed."

"Except you."

"Except me."

"My sentiments exactly."

"I just want to keep kissing you. I can't get enough of your mouth."

"Be my guest. And in future I'll wear buttons in front."

Every night this week you've had a sweet hour with Julie. Every night you've held her small breasts in your hands while her tongue presses against yours. Now it's Friday.

"Do you want to make love?"

"Yes."

"Is there anywhere?"

"There's plenty of bush."

"Let's lose ourselves in the bush."

"Yes."

"Tomorrow?"

"Yes."

You are lying in bed, thinking about tomorrow. A big moon is outside the window and a breeze is making the leafy branch move gently against the glass. The movement is like the motion of lovemaking. You get out of bed to look at it. The lake is lit with moonlight and the stars overhead and the lights on the distant shore are all pulsating. You wonder if there is a single word which could mean so much beauty. The word is *Julie*.

And now you are seeing the sun's orange blaze through closed eyelids. The sun is on your body and on the long grass flattened around you. You could float out of your body now, except your body feels too good to leave. Your nipple tickles and

The Cure

you open an eye. Julie is sitting naked beside you, playing with a grass stem. She leans to kiss you.

"You're so beautiful," you tell her. "It makes me want to die."

"Don't die."

"This was my first time," you confess.

"I wouldn't have known. You're awfully good at it."

"Was it nice for you, really?"

"Yes, you horny devil!"

"Let's do it again!"

"You'll have to ask me nicely," she says. "I'm just a modest maiden." Then she takes your rising prick in her mouth.

We are kissing in the shadows outside your ward.

"I can't bear to leave you."

"I don't want to either."

"Tomorrow won't be long."

"No."

"We'll go to the bush."

"Yes please."

"Will you be a modest maiden again?"

"If you'll be a horny devil."

"I love you."

"I love you."

You get into the dining room just in time. It's the same as always, but now you don't mind the noise and stink and madness. Nothing can touch you. You just wish you could use your own wonderful luck like a wand and touch these wretches and light them up.

A screw comes to your table with the medication tray. He gives Stark his dose, then Stern and Gilroy. He hands you some blue tablets.

"I'm not on medication," you say, smiling. This mistake sometimes happens.

"Yes you are. The doctor's put you on it."

In your head an image: a gigantic black snake, lunging from the sweet grass.

10

You deserve it. For being so stupid. For thinking you could ever come in from the cold wastes of the world of *The Survivor*. In those wastes there are no hopes and only the worst can happen, and when it does happen you are ready for it. When you leave that world you immediately take on hopes which disarm you. Or if you let yourself have hopes they must be tiny ones, ones so close to being nothing that they can't hurt you much. The thing with Julie was too big, stupidly big, so you deserve whatever will happen now.

When the meal is finished you file out with the others and get through The Gauntlet—though it doesn't matter now—and go into the dayroom and sit alone in the alcove. You are trying to feel whether you feel different yet and wondering how the effects will come. The blue tablets are Stelazine. You know from seeing others they can have very bad side effects. You picture various men you've known who became slobbering zombies. Barry Clarke was like that in MAX. He dribbled green slime.

After a couple of hours you begin to feel strange. A sort of restlessness is on you, making it hard to sit still. You walk across the alcove but you immediately feel weak and must sit again. As soon as you sit the restlessness comes back. By bedtime you feel very bad.

It is impossible to rest. It has nothing to do with sleeping. You couldn't sleep properly in the dormitory before anyway. Now you can't even bear to lie prone because the restlessness is too much. You think perhaps if you do some push-ups you might be able to tire yourself out, so you go into the shower room and try it. After two push-ups your energy is gone and you have to stop. You lie in bed again, then try more push-ups, then lie down for another few minutes, then try push-ups again. The two forces are exactly balanced—restlessness and lack of energy.

Morning takes years to come. You have to force yourself to sit still at the table. You feel so weak the spoon seems heavy as lead. They give you more Stelazine. You're to have it three times daily.

You go to your spot at the side and try to read, to return to David Allison and the cold muddy wastes, but you've no concentration. You put the book aside, take it up, put it down. You had arranged to meet Julie at the canteen at nine-thirty. You aren't going. To see her would only start you crying or something. Anyway, it's all different now.

Just after nine-thirty the thought of Julie overcomes everything and you go to the canteen. It seems a long way and you must keep stopping to gather your strength. She isn't there. You are almost glad. You sit by the water till it seems lunchtime, but you find it isn't even ten-thirty. Time can't drag this slowly, it's impossible. The thought of Julie is powerful again, so you make your way, slowly, like an old man, to a part of the road where you can see Admission. She doesn't come. You are almost glad. Better it ends this way.

They give you more tablets at lunchtime and now the effects are building to full strength. You hobble to the canteen after lunch, then to the place where you might see her coming from Admission. The only thing that could make this bearable would be if you knew that when the day ended, years and years from now, you could sleep. But all that will happen is that years and years of night will start.

OT isn't a refuge any more, not from this. You can't stay at the sewing machine for more than a minute and must get up to fiddle with some other job, then the weakness drains you and you sink into the chair again for another minute. You tell Con Pappas about the Stelazine. Just the fact of it. It isn't a thing you can describe properly to anyone.

Cheryl and Janice know you are on this medication and can see you aren't too happy. But they are nurses and part of their job is to make things like this happen to people. If they really understood how you feel they'd have to understand that their job is partly cruel and wicked, and you can't expect them to do that. Mr Trowbridge thinks the Stelazine is a mistake, not because it's cruel and wicked but because Work is the best medication.

"There's usually a period of discomfort before you become stabilised," he tells you. "Two to three weeks."

But you can't grasp normal time any more. Two to three weeks will hardly get you to the end of today.

Going back from OT you hear her call. She's walking quickly along from Admission.

"What's wrong?" she asks, looking at you.

"Nothing."

"Are you mad at me?"

"No."

"Yes you are. You think I'm a bitch for not meeting you yesterday."

"It doesn't matter."

"My parents came. I couldn't get away. Truly."

"It doesn't matter."

"I *felt* like a bitch, if that's any consolation to you."

"You aren't."

"Truly?"

"Truly."

"D'you want to have a walk now? Look, buttons all in front."

She's so sweet, so kind. You just want her to go away and leave you in the cold wastes.

"I can't go for a walk."

"Is something really wrong?"

"It doesn't matter."

"What doesn't?"

"I can't see you any more."

There is a long silence. You are staring at the ground.

"I get the message."

"There isn't any message."

"You used me!"

"No," you say. You don't want her to think that. "If I'd just used you I'd try to use you some more, wouldn't I?"

"Then you're tired of me!"

"No."

"God, I haven't any tabs on myself, but I thought I could satisfy a man for longer than a week!"

"You're a wonderful person."

"That's a bloody easy thing to say!"

You have no energy left. Standing here has sapped you.

"I have to go inside now."

"Len," she says in a softer tone. "Are you sick? You look it."

"No, I just can't see you any more."

"Just like that?" Her voice is hard again.

When you are heading into the cold wastes it doesn't matter what anyone thinks of you. It's better and simpler, really, if they hate you. But you don't want any of the hate to rub off on her. You don't want her to think this is happening because of something wrong with her. There's one more thing you can say.

"I'm doing Life. You know that. Sooner or later, in a few weeks, you'll have to go away. I'd rather have the break now while I can still stand it. If I'm with you for a few more weeks I won't be able to."

"Christ, is that all? I could keep seeing you! Every weekend!"

"No."

"We'd still be together!"

"I have to go inside now."

"Wait a minute!"

"I have to go in." You walk away, with your last bit of energy.

"You're a liar!" she calls after you. "I was a handy fuck, wasn't I! Well fuck *you*!"

You think she is crying. A thought comes. It might be important if you had the energy to examine it. Maybe all the stuff about the cold wastes is a way for you to kill the ideas of things, kill them symbolically in your mind—love and optimism and innocence and other things. You pretend you're a victim. Maybe you are really a kind of sadist.

It's been a week. You have tried to talk to the Charge Sister but your mouth has gone peculiar. You can say a few words okay, then you get a sensation like lockjaw and if you try to speak any more the words begin to sound like a retard's grunts. If you try to speak to the screws and nurses they look at you as if they can't imagine what could possibly be wrong apart from there being something wrong with your mind. You manage to ask the Charge Sister why you're on Stelazine.

"The doctor noticed you in the grounds one day and decided you required extra help."

"But why?"

"Better ask the doctor."

Of course it's because of the lovemaking. It has to be. You've done nothing else wrong. You don't bother asking "The German". In Group Therapy you hold yourself rigid in the chair, trying to seem composed. You try to get at the back of the group where "The German" won't notice you so much. But you mustn't appear to be hiding or she might pay you extra attention. When she asks you a question you answer as much like a bright five-year-old as possible, so she'll be satisfied and not press you. If you had to say very much your jaw would seize up and you'd be grunting.

It's been two weeks. You are at the waterfront on Sunday morning, lying with your face pressed into the grass. You are counting seconds. Counting seconds is a way of keeping a slight grip on things. You count sixty and another minute is over, then count again and you've got through another minute. If you could do it sixty times you'd be through a whole hour, but you can't concentrate for more than three or four sixties and must get up and walk about until the weakness drains you and you sink down again to count some more.

Someone comes past. It's one of the Admission patients Julie introduced you to at the film night.

"Hi," he says.

You don't want to answer in case he stops and wants to talk. You can't talk to anyone now. But you need to ask him something.

"Hi," you say, looking up. "How's Julie?"

"Oh, she left," he says. "Got herself discharged the other day."

You bury your face in the grass so he'll go away.

Walking back to the ward you feel a sensation like goose pimples in your legs. Your legs won't move properly. You stop by the roadside and the feeling goes. After you've gone another little way it comes back and you have to stop again. The feeling now is a bit like the feeling when your jaw seizes up. Your legs are paralysed. You wonder if this is how polio begins, or some other disease like that. You are terribly frightened. You hobble to the ward with many stops and starts and tell the Charge Sister what has happened. It's hard to tell her because of your mouth going peculiar. She's busy and hasn't time to listen properly, but you manage to make her understand what your grunts mean.

"It's just a side effect of Stelazine," she says. "It isn't uncommon."

You can't go to OT because of your legs, so you stay on the courtyard, counting seconds, for a few days. It's hard even to walk into the dining room. You hobble a few paces in and then must grip the nearest table and stay there trying to keep your balance until the paralysis eases a bit and you can hobble a few more steps to your chair. A screw sees you acting this way and tells you to get to your place quick smart. You can't explain because your mouth has gone peculiar again. The screw tries to frogmarch you across the room but your legs won't stay under you and you fall over and bump a table. The screw thinks you are just being difficult in an idiot retard way and is ready to thump you. After that the Charge Sister says you can have your meals on a tray in the dayroom if you wish, though that would obviously be a nuisance for the staff. Her tone indicates just how much of a nuisance it would be, and also that you seem to be playing on your condition at least a teeny bit and could pull yourself together if you tried. So you keep hobbling into the dining room and the screws and nurses are fairly tolerant.

The paralysis stops after four days and you go to OT again, though you still can't work properly because of the restlessness and weakness alternating every half-minute or so. You ought to be stabilising on the medication now but it's as bad as ever.

You are writing to your mother, asking her to come and help you. Your writing is all squiggly and crazy. What will she think if she gets a letter that looks as if it was written by a madman? And you can't concentrate well enough to frame what you need to say.

You understand you are in another of the brilliant traps. If you claim the doctor is treating you wrongly or cruelly you have a persecution complex. And if you aren't claiming that then there's no point saying anything at all. You try to make the letter sound reasonable but urgent. That doesn't alter the trap of course. If you are being reasonable it shows the Stelazine is doing you good. If you aren't being reasonable it shows you need the Stelazine to help you *become* reasonable.

Your mother comes up from the city and asks to see the doctor.

"Doctor's busy just now," says the Charge Sister. "But I'll be glad to answer any queries you may have."

We go into the Charge Sister's office and sit down. The Charge Sister looks very matronly in her starched white veil.

"I'm a bit worried about this medicine Len is getting," your mother says.

"What's the trouble?"

"Len tells me it has a bad effect on him."

"Oh, most medication has some side effects."

"He tells me he was paralysed."

"That does sometimes happen, but it passes off quickly."

"I see," says your mother. The Charge Sister's veil is very white and shining.

"Any other worries?" asks the Charge Sister. She's glad to be able to lay this simple woman's anxieties to rest.

Your mother is trying to maintain the tone of a concerned parent and taxpayer who means to get to the bottom of this. It must seem pathetic to the Charge Sister.

"Just what *is* this stuff Len is on?"

"Stelazine? Oh, an excellent medication. We use it extensively."

"I see. And why is Len getting this Stel … er, Steltazone?"

"Stelazine," the Charge Sister corrects.

"Sorry, Stelazine."

"Well, Doctor felt Len was rather *withdrawn* and needed extra support."

That "withdrawn" is odd. Making love with a girl isn't being "withdrawn"!

Your mother doesn't know what more to say, but she wants to show you she is sticking up for you.

"Len always was a quiet boy."

"Of course. But Doctor felt that Len needed extra support, you see, to improve his social interaction."

"Well, none of our family is very outgoing." Your mother is casting about in her mind for an illustration. "I mean, well, for instance, there are times when I just won't answer the phone."

"That isn't quite *normal* behaviour, though, is it?"

You shouldn't have got your mother into this. She's a babe in the woods. They'll have *her* on Stelazine in a minute. You make a movement to interrupt.

Your mother must catch her train. Before she goes she tells you not to worry and that everything will be alright. She almost tells you the doctor knows best, but checks herself. You understand her position. Relatives need to think that way and it's a kindness to let them.

What the Charge Sister said about you being too withdrawn must mean they didn't even know about Julie. You are getting Stelazine not because they know you had sex with a girl but because they didn't know. It doesn't really matter why you're getting it. You just are. If it wasn't for one reason it'd be for the exact opposite reason. That's how the system works.

Thinking about all that takes too much energy. You go back to counting seconds. Cars often pass you on the road while you're hobbling to or from OT and you begin to dwell on how easy it would be to step in front of one of them. You even begin to brace yourself when a car is approaching. But you might only be injured, or crippled. That wouldn't solve anything. You'd need to be sure of being killed outright. And something else stops you: the knowledge that the system would have an easy explanation of your suicide. Poor deranged Tarbutt! If only he'd responded to treatment!

You are at OT, a month after the Stelazine began. Mr Trowbridge notices you are on the verge of breaking down. Your work has gone to pot.

"How d'you feel within yourself, Len?"

"I can't stand it any more!"

"You don't appear to be stabilising, that's for sure."

"I can't stand it any more!"

"Have you spoken to your ward doctor?"

"Yes, she asked me how many fucking dwarfs Snow White had and I told her the answer and she was very fucking pleased with me!"

"Mmmmm ... I can see you're under a bit of strain."

"Oh we mustn't overstate the fucking matter! I just have a strong urge to kill my fucking self, that's all!"

"Come with me," says Mr Trowbridge.

We go out past Cheryl and Janice, who are both looking at you very seriously from their end of the room, up past REFRACT to the Administration block. You have to hobble fast to keep up.

"I'll speak to the Medical Superintendent," Mr Trowbridge says.

"What's he got to do with it?"

"He ordered the Stelazine for you. Didn't you know?"

We go into the Administration block and Mr Trowbridge goes in past a secretary to the Superintendent's office. After a minute he calls you in. The Superintendent is peering across a desk. He has very bad breath. It fills up the room. This bad breath is famous. Everyone knows about it but him.

"I gather you aren't very happy," he says.

"The medication is unsuitable."

"Len isn't stabilising," says Mr Trowbridge.

"We could try him on Melleril perhaps."

"And I'd suggest a change of ward also," says Mr Trowbridge.

"Ward 24's awful," you say, trying not to whine. "They're turning me into a retard!"

The Superintendent stares at you. He has glasses on and the lenses are blank and bright. He looks inhuman.

"Let's say a transfer to REHAB, as well as the change to Melleril," Mr Trowbridge prompts.

"Alright," murmurs the Superintendent. "We'll agree to that then, shall we, Len?"

"Yes," you say, as though your agreement matters, as though nobody here would dream of forcing anything on you. On the way back to OT you thank Mr Trowbridge. You want to tell him he can count on your help if he ever needs it. That's just an emotional impulse. If inmates were able to help anyone, even themselves, they wouldn't be inmates.

At lunchtime you are given a brown tablet instead of the blue ones, and after lunch the Charge Sister tells you to get your gear from the storeroom. A nurse will take you to REHAB. As you go along the corridor you sniff the stink of newness for the last time. The stink is mingled now, after three months, with a permanent reek of shit and piss.

The nurse walks down the slope from the courtyard and towards the area where the Admission wards are. REHAB is near there, on a sort of plateau that overlooks the lake from a different angle and lower down than the high hill of Ward 24. You follow the nurse. She doesn't speak, and you've nothing to say. A car approaches along the road. The nurse turns and takes you by the sleeve and draws you to the side until the car is past. You let yourself be pulled. She's just doing her job, keeping a retard from getting run over. You don't want to be run over either. Not now.

11

REHAB's full name is Rehabilitation & Resocialisation Unit. That's painted in big letters over the entrance. Most wards are called Units now and have big words over the entrances. It doesn't matter what the words are, so long as they look good.

The nurse takes you into the office and leaves you with a screw on duty there. He sends you into the dayroom. After a while a bloke comes and says his name is Cecil and he's on the Patients' Committee and will show you where to put your gear and where your bed is and stuff like that. Cecil is scrawny and has asthma or something and gasps after the exertion of walking up a corridor to the storeroom.

"Which space?" you ask him. The storeroom has shelves with numbered spaces.

"Er, 17, I think."

You find 17 and put your gear there.

"Is that 17?" Cecil asks.

"Yep."

The spaces have numbers taped on the front but 17's tape has come off. Cecil looks confused. You point out that your space has sixteen on one side and eighteen on the other. Cecil looks very worried.

"I'd better go and ask about it," he says.

"Why bother?"

"I don't want any trouble," he says.

"Why would there be trouble?"

"Blue's on tomorrow," he says, as if that explained it all.

"Who is Blue?"

But Cecil has a coughing fit and begins choking. He drools a pool of spit on the floor. He hurries for a mop. Later he shows you your bed. The dormitory is like the one in Ward 24 but tidier and without the new smell.

"Listen," you say, "what's this Patients' Committee?"

"A sort of committee of patients."

"I thought it might be," you say. "But what does it do?"

"We sort of help organise things, like ward duties and that."

"And who's this Blue that you mentioned?"

Cecil begins coughing again. His eyes go wide, like those of a scared rabbit.

It's too late to go to OT so you wander around the ward. There are three little groups in the dayroom, each with half a dozen patients seated with a nurse. The nurses have newspapers and are reading items out aloud and trying to get the patients to comment. A group of patients is outside raking the lawn, with screws and nurses watching. None of these inmates are obvious retards, just run-of-the-mill types, men and women, shabby, submissive. The screw in charge of the raking barks orders. You try not to make yourself too visible. You still feel pretty bad from the last dose of Stelazine. It'll be twenty-four hours or so before the effects really begin to wane. And you don't know, yet, what the brown Melleril pill has in store for you. Mr Trowbridge said Melleril is quite mild. That's just his opinion. You'd bet your boots he's never swallowed one.

The group comes inside from the lawn and other patients come back from work-places and by evening the dayroom is full. Most are watching TV. There is a card game happening in a corner. One of the card players is the fattest person, for her size, that you've ever seen. She is very short and her feet don't quite touch the floor, but the fat of her backside hangs in folds over the sides of her chair and the fat of her arms spreads in rolls on the table. She holds the cards close to her eyes with little sausage fingers. She has a little prim, self-important voice.

"What's trumps?" she asks.

"Spades is trumps. Wake up and listen!"

"You needn't be unpleasant."

"You'd give anyone the shits, Christine!"

"I'll report you in the Ward Meeting if you aren't careful. I don't want to but I have a duty."

"Stick it!"

"I'm on the Committee, you know."

"Stick it!"

The annoyed player leaves the table.

"I'm glad he's gone," the fat girl tells the remaining two. "I'd have to report him otherwise. That's the worst of Committee work—the responsibility." She sighs deeply, then seems to doze, her chin on the edge of the table and the cards still in her hand.

The meal is called and we enter the dining room. There are three green-uniformed pantrymaids on duty, dishing food out of dixies and pushing plates across the servery. Each row of tables is called up in turn. There's a lot of noise, mostly from the two younger pantrymaids who keep shrieking at us. When a row is called up and we respond a moment too soon a pantrymaid screams for us to wait till we're bloodywell called. If we respond a moment late she screams for us to get off our bloody arses. The screw in charge of the dining room strides among the tables and snarls, as though we are giving the pantrymaids a hard time and had better cut it out.

A nurse brings the medication tray and you are given your Melleril tablet. You put it under your tongue and pretend to swallow. We have been in the dining room for nine and a half minutes, according to the clock on the wall, and the meal is over. Only the fat girl Christine is still eating, pushing the last bits of food into her mouth with fat little fingers. She's eaten no more than the rest, it's just that her fat little mouth and hands can't work fast enough.

The loudest pantrymaid comes and stands with hands on hips.

"Get a bloody move on! We're not stayin' here all friggin' night for *you*!"

Christine looks up, chewing like a little cow.

"Bugger you then!" snaps the pantrymaid, and whips the plate away.

As we file out the door a nurse taps you on the arm.

"Mrs Fibbitson wants to know if you'll help wash up."

You look back at the servery and see the senior pantrymaid has her eye on you.

"Alright," you say. You haven't much choice. And it's a bit awkward because you want to hurry to the lavatory and get rid of the tablet. It's starting to disintegrate in your mouth.

Mrs Fibbitson points you to a big sink with a pile of dirty dixies. You go to it and are able to spit the tablet down the plughole before you begin washing up. When you've finished and have wiped the sink and counter Mrs Fibbitson asks if you'll be a regular pantry helper. The job's main perk is extra food, but you're more interested in the fact that pantry helpers have their meal a few minutes before the others, so you'd be able to eat when the dining room is empty and quiet. And afterwards you'll have your head over the sink with the banging dixies and won't have to hear the abuse so much. That plughole will be handy too.

The dayroom has a snooker table in an alcove on one side and an area on the other side with a sliding partition to close it off from the rest of the room. You sit behind the partition.

"Got any skins?" says a voice beside you. There's a gaunt bloke in the next chair.

"Pardon?"

"Skins. Got any?"

"What kind of skins?"

"Sheepskins."

"No."

"Cowhides?"

"No."

"Goatskins? Horseskins?"

"No."

"I'll pay."

"I haven't any."

"What about dogskins?"

"No."

The gaunt man is leaning over, gazing at you intently.

"You're keeping them for yourself, aren't you?"

"I haven't any."

"I understand. You won't part with them. I expected as much. But I need new patches urgently, you see. For my arm and also just here on the thigh." He shows you his arm and pulls his shirt up to let you see his upper thigh. "The bones are almost through in both places. The left shoulderblade will be through any day as well."

"You look okay to me," you say.

"Oh, I appreciate your position. You've your own needs to consider. But if you do find you have some extra skins I hope you'll let me know. Remember, I'll pay."

The gaunt man is being so reasonable about it all you half-think to give him a skin or two. You stay sitting with your back to the partition, watching other patients, listening to the talk, thinking what a change, after Ward 24, to be in a place where there's at least one reasonable person.

The night is okay, with only the normal smells and noises of a dormitory. Cecil has an asthma attack in the night, but nothing else happens. Coming downstairs in the morning you hear loud voices in the corridor. A frowsy woman patient runs into sight at the foot of the stairs. She's looking over her shoulder and shouting something about her children. She seems to be crying but she has a bad smoker's cough and it's hard to tell if she's really crying or merely trying to shout and cough at the same time. You pause on the stairs. A nurse runs into sight and grabs the woman and shoves her against the wall and yells into her ear that her children are better off without her because she's a mad old bitch and not a fit mother for a cat. The patient is twisting her head away and screwing her face up as though she doesn't want to hear. The nurse says very coolly into the woman's ear that it doesn't matter anyway because she's been booked for shock treatment and soon won't remember her children or anyone else. The nurse has very red hair and a ruddy, healthy complexion like a farmer's wife. She wears the starched veil of a senior Sister. She looks up and notices you on the stairs. You walk down casually as if you haven't noticed anything and pass by them to the courtyard. You know this Sister must be Blue.

Calisthenics are held every morning on the courtyard and all patients must do them. Nurses and screws go through the ward prodding patients out to the centre where they must line up and do bends and jerks and stuff like that. You don't mind calisthenics. It's good to stretch in the fresh morning with the lake and sky so vast and clean around you. The exercises are led by Syd Hicks, a loudmouth who's on the Patients' Committee with Cecil. Christine can't bend or jerk because of her fat, so she does vague hand movements to show she's in the spirit of it. After the first couple of minutes you decide you don't like these calisthenics. All the young screws and nurses are lounging along the verandah, watching us and joking about Christine's fat or Cecil's wheezing. Cecil tries to drop out of the line to rest but a nurse called Wanda tells him it's no use bunging on an act and orders him back. The Skin Man finds the exercises distressing too. He's afraid the exertion will make his bones poke through his skin. You think how grotesque we must look—fat girls and asthmatics and broken-down inmates all trying to bend and jerk in a row.

As soon as it's over you slip away to your early breakfast and then go gladly to the sink with the banging dixies which drown out some of the shouted abuse in the dining room. Then you escape to OT.

12

You take a longer route back from OT each evening now. Instead of cutting across the paddock where the kangaroos browse you walk along another loop of road by the lake shore and then up a very long hill past Admission and so to REHAB. Usually the setting sun is poised at the top of the hill and seems to be resting on the bitumen. You get a blaze of light in your eyes and the road ahead is fiery with it. You've christened that long hill Glory Road.

You wander freely at weekends and have discovered lovely places. There is a field near the main kitchen where cows from the hospital dairy graze. There's a peacefulness about cows. At weekends you take a book and sit under a tree near the field and read a little and listen to music on your transistor and watch the cows. Sometimes you lean on the fence and click your tongue at the cows and they will wander close and sniff at you and examine you with big peaceful eyes but with a dubious look also, as if they're wondering what your game is. You don't stay leaning on the fence too long. It's a bit too visible there. It might look odd. Other people don't spend their time looking at cattle. Looking at cattle is probably a symptom of something. It's safer under the tree where you are shielded.

The pond below OT is another good place. Often you find hundreds of ducks on the water, and some swans, and herons stalking about the mudflats on their stilty legs, and shags holding their wings open in the sun. The hospital is full of birds. The cows even have their own detachment of cattle egrets, white birds which fuss about amongst the herd like junior assistants who are cleverer than their bosses and take care of details in the grass which the big slow-thinkers overlook.

There is a row of beautiful willows near the pond. You read somewhere that willows were anciently associated with magic and with poetry, so every time you pass them you say a little charm that you've devised:

Willow, Willow, poets' tree,
Shed thy willow grace on me.

***

You take to carrying a willow twig in your pocket. You fancy its magic will protect you and its poetry rub off on you. The urge to poetry has been coming back lately. The beauty and eternity of birds and animals and trees have revived it.

Instead of Group Therapy sessions REHAB has a Ward Meeting twice a week. Everyone attends, patients, staff, and usually the doctor. The doctor's name is Muckerjee and he wears a turban. You don't see much of him except at Ward Meetings where he sits listening and nodding his head whenever the staff say anything. He nods especially hard when Blue speaks.

The Ward Meeting has a set pattern. First the Patients' Committee reports on the ward chores. Cecil invariably just says that everything's okay on the male side. He's too nervous to report anyone for slacking. Christine always has a list of complaints about the females: how Beryl Wrigley forgot to sweep the stairs or how Elsie Haggart didn't mop the bathroom properly. Elsie Haggart is the frowsy one with the children she soon won't remember because of shock treatment, and Christine knows that Blue likes hearing complaints about Elsie Haggart. It disgusts you the way these patients dob each other in. In MAX it was almost unheard of. In MAX the blokes had a code, and if you felt the force of the code slipping and felt tempted to dob your mates in there was always the possibility of getting a knife in your belly to reinforce your conscience. Christine keeps a notebook of the faults and failures of patients and when her turn comes at the Ward Meeting she reads her notebook out in her prim little voice, sighing repeatedly to show how sorry she is to have to do it. Of course she must be woken first. Waking Christine is a ritual joke. When the moment comes all eyes go to the dozing fat girl, then Blue says quietly: "And now we will have the privilege of hearing from…" and then she screams "CHRISTINE!" The fat girl wobbles awake, blinks, and reaches for the notebook.

The next stage is for Blue to give her own views on the ward chores. Reprisals are threatened if things don't improve. Then

Blue and other staff go on to more general matters of discipline. Lack of enthusiasm for calisthenics is a regular issue. Reprisals are threatened. Blue asks Christine what the reprisal ought to be this time. Christine screws up her fat face and thinks hard and suggests stopping all inmates' TV viewing for a week. Blue approves. It adds a nice touch if the punishment is devised by one of the victims. Christine basks in her moment of importance. Our harassment of the pantrymaids is a standard issue also. Reprisals are threatened.

After this we are invited to voice any problems we may have. Someone says his medication is having bad side effects and describes the nausea and giddiness. Blue tells him that nausea and giddiness are not, and never were, side effects of that particular medication. The patient is either lying or grossly disturbed. Shock may be required. Dr Muckerjee nods solemnly. Blue asks if anyone else wants to complain about medication. Nobody does. The meeting ends.

Elsie Haggart has had her withdrawal stopped for two weeks. Each Friday patients are allowed to draw a couple of dollars from their accounts to spend at the canteen, and having this money stopped is called Negative Reinforcement. Elsie Haggart is a heavy smoker and can't buy her week's tobacco. We are forbidden to give her a smoke. You are in the dayroom, in a spot where you can see along the corridor. Blue is there, whispering with the nurse Wanda who is her closest henchman. Wanda comes into the dayroom and sits beside Elsie Haggart and lights a cigarette. Wanda leans back, drawing deeply on the fag and blowing the smoke at Elsie Haggart. Elsie is gripping the arms of the chair, her frowsy face tight and white. The nurse keeps blowing the smoke until the cigarette is finished.

Elsie Haggart makes it ridiculously easy, especially by harping all the time about her children. She lives only for a visit or a message from them. You are near Elsie on the courtyard one day when Wanda comes and tells her very gently that the children are on the phone. Elsie Haggart is too distraught and probably too stupid to be on her guard. She runs to the office. You are standing near the window of a spare office across the corridor. You hear Elsie Haggart shrieking "My darlings! Are you there?" into the phone. Then Blue's voice, silken, into the phone in the other office: "Yes, I'm here, Elsie. I'm always here."

Elsie Haggart is locked up until her hysteria has passed and next morning gets electroshock.

Electroshock is given in the male dormitory, on one of the beds after a rubber sheet has been laid down and other equipment assembled around it. Patients booked for shock wait in a small room nearby. They are taken in turn and those still left can hear the moans and pleadings and the buzz of the machine.

You get on fairly well with Blue. You've studied her. You've seen that she is provoked by vulnerability, like some wild animal which isn't very dangerous unless you stumble and expose your throat. If she sees you aren't afraid and aren't liable to stumble she becomes almost pleasant. You must be careful though. You never know how you might stumble, or when. Being Mrs Fibbitson's main pantry helper is a safeguard. Mrs Fibbitson is a dour old stick but she appreciates an inmate who'll wash dixies efficiently day in and day out, and her opinion carries weight in REHAB.

Since Ward 24 you have grasped something important. If you make yourself useful it will suit the staff's convenience to leave you alone. Electroshock or severe medication interfere with an inmate's usefulness. In Ward 24 you thought they should leave you alone just because you were a person with rights and feelings. That was foolish. Your other big mistake was retreating into silence. You thought they'd see it as your protest against being insulted to the very core. But naturally they took it as proof of illness. They were offering psychiatric care and you were flinching from it, the way a possessed man would flinch from holy water. It's safer to speak up, providing you are careful. So now you make a point of talking to a few screws and nurses each day — about football or the weather, it doesn't matter what—to show you are in touch with reality. Their reality at least. And you speak up in Ward Meetings. You make at least one comment in each meeting. Mostly it's about ward chores, like how you noticed the dormitory broom is worn out and could we have a new one. That sort of comment is good. It shows you are taking an interest, playing your part as a member of this Therapeutic Community.

Sometimes you even help other inmates to speak up: "I think what Stan is trying to say..." You mustn't sound like a barracks lawyer though.

Elsie Haggart is finished the course of shock and is back to normal. She's making a fuss in the Ward Meeting, complaining that she's lost contact with her children. Blue tells her to be quiet. Elsie gets more excited. She's babbling something about Blue persecuting her. She's on thin ice. Blue doesn't really care what Elsie Haggart says, but it's slightly awkward her saying it in front of the doctor and all the other staff. As a member of the Therapeutic Community it saddens you to see a fellow inmate in the grip of persecution delusions. You speak up:

"Perhaps if contact were restored with the children, Elsie might begin to get her ideas into normal perspective."

"They don't write!" moans Elsie.

"Well, do you write to *them*?" Blue wants to know. Blue doesn't feel that weeks as an electroshocked zombie need interfere with letter writing.

"I can't write very good," says Elsie. In fact she can't write at all except to sign her name.

The obvious thing would be for someone to help Elsie write a letter once a week, but nobody wants to get involved in her problems. You certainly don't. Elsie Haggart is a pain in the neck. You make another suggestion:

"Maybe Elsie could buy a postcard at the canteen each week and post it home. Ones with nice pictures the children would like. It'd be something at least."

The canteen sells lovely postcards. Lake scenes with pelicans, and kangaroos with joeys peeping out.

Elsie Haggart mutters agreement. She's calmer now that someone is taking her part. Blue is considering. She's aware that she could make a small concession in return for the persecution talk being cooled. And the concession would be to you, not Elsie.

"But Elsie is off withdrawals. How would she buy postcards?" Blue wants to know.

You put on a perplexed expression, as though this is a major stumbling block, as though being off withdrawals is an act of God or something.

"Well," you say, "what if withdrawals could somehow be restored, on the understanding that Elsie improves her behaviour?"

Blue considers again. Dr Muckerjee has been nodding and listening. He probably hasn't followed it too well because of his limited English, but he murmurs to Blue that it seems fair.

So Blue agrees.

The postcard idea won't work, except for a week or two, and Elsie Haggart will be off withdrawals again very soon. It's nothing to you.

You are on the Patients' Committee now in Cecil's place. Cecil was too timid for the job and wouldn't report other patients. Not like Christine with her notebook. Being off the committee hasn't helped Cecil's nervousness though because now he's afraid Blue will start on him for having proved so useless. Each morning before breakfast you go around and check whether the chores on the male side have been done. If something isn't done you go to the person and remind him. If he still doesn't do it you report him. At first you tried to cover for people by doing some of the chores yourself, but it got too much. Now you figure if people are too stupid to keep out of trouble it's not your concern. Besides, one or two bad reports at each Ward Meeting keep Blue happy.

Syd Hicks has been chucked off the committee also and you are leading the calisthenics in his place. You are getting to be Blue's golden-haired boy these days. You and she understand each other, like two people who understand the rules of a secret game.

Con Pappas has been transferred to REHAB and he thinks all his birthdays have come at once.

13

Your policy of being sociable with the staff interferes a lot with your writing. Lots of times when you want to be outside under the sky with your own thoughts you are playing snooker with some screw instead, or talking about football or playing cards. You are freer at OT and can daydream while you sew the vinyl bags, but you have to keep your quota up or Mr Trowbridge might get the idea you aren't as well as you ought to be. Apart from weekends, the main time for thinking about poetry is on your evening wander back to REHAB. It's a lovely time, perhaps because it only lasts an hour, including the stop at the canteen and another stop at the lake, and so every minute seems precious. The day is just turning cool then and the shadows are lengthening and there is an evening breeze to ruffle the water and the trees and dry the sweat from you as you come to the top of Glory Road. Or if the day is wet you walk in the rain in an old overcoat and enjoy the different scene that the rain makes, when the lake is like wrinkled iron and the grass and trees and buildings are plastered with water and the roadway and gutters stream with it.

You have begun to think a lot about this hospital. Before, you thought mainly about your own experience of it or about inmates you've observed or known. Now every evening when you reach the top of Glory Road you look across at the hospital spread out on the slopes and wonder what this place really is, what it's for, how it came to be. It has a history and customs and laws and a government. People come here and exist for a while and then die or go away. This place is like a town with its generations that pass by, but stranger than a town because no-one is born here and no-one marries. The only important human event that ever happens here is death. Mr Trowbridge started you thinking this way when he set up a paper-shredding section at OT, with a big machine that chops newspapers and other papers into ribbons which are then baled and sent away on a truck. The Records Office sent dozens of boxes of old files. It took three days to shred them. You browsed among the boxes, reading the yellowed folders that gave off puffs of stale dust. Each folder told of someone who was here forty or sixty years ago. Forty or sixty years ago someone was here, alive, and the sun and wind and grass and water were as real for them as for you now. It has given you a sort of ache to understand how lives can be sucked back and dried and silenced into folders, the folders stamped *Cancelled*, and then shredded to nothing. You began making notes for a poem.

It took a while to see the theme clearly. At first it was to be a sort of history of the hospital and what has happened here through all the years those yellowed folders represented. Then you saw it. The poem would be a series of dialogues between the files and the shredder, each file, each life, giving its last testimony as its turn came. And the shredder, remorseless but not cruel, holding its sharp blades ready until each testimony was told.

Sam Lister and his beautiful wife have come to see you. Sam was with you in MAX years ago. You are walking with them by the lake and you and Sam are remembering the times then when the two of you talked and talked—about happiness, and the meaning of life, and whether we'd be free some day and things like that. Sam is still the same, though there is the slight embarrassment between you now because he is free and you aren't yet. And Sam's wife is as beautiful as you remember her from the times she visited Sam in MAX. She walks along a little apart from the two of us, shy of intruding on memories she isn't part of. Later we sit behind a wall out of the wind and eat sandwiches and talk some more. You show them the poem. Sam reads the fifteen closely written pages, not saying anything, then passes them to his beautiful lady and she reads them and doesn't say anything for a long time either. You stare away into the wind, wondering if you've made a mistake. Then they both tell you, quietly and feelingly, that it's the best poem they've ever read. You are very pleased that two people you like so much like your poem, but you have that odd feeling of wanting to change the subject so you won't seem to be making a big deal of your work.

"Will you have it published?" asks Sam's lady.

"Easier said than done," you say.

"It ought to be published," Sam insists.

"Yes," says his beautiful lady. "I want a copy of it."

"Take that copy, if you like. I have another."

"Are you sure?"

"Yes, take it. I'd like you and Sam to have it."

Sam's lady folds the poem carefully and puts it in her bag. She leans and kisses you lightly on the cheek. Whacko, you think to yourself, that's the stuff to give the troops! You walk back to the car with them. They seem sad and quiet. You act cheerful and wave them off with a big smile. As soon as the car goes out of sight loneliness drops on you like a ton weight.

The staff are on strike. They don't like the new Medical Superintendent who has replaced the one with the famous bad breath. Dr Grey sat in on a Ward Meeting soon after he came. It was an awful shock, especially for Blue. Dr Grey didn't sit quietly nodding like Dr Muckerjee, instead he looked very alert and he talked to the inmates as though we were really quite intelligent. He said we should help ourselves more and not rely on the staff to run our lives. At first Blue smirked and made faces to the other nurses, as though to say they might as well let this fool have his foibles. When the Skin Man got up and said about needing skins to patch himself with, Blue told him to sit down and shut up. Dr Grey overruled her briskly and invited the Skin Man to continue. Then he explained to him very carefully that he didn't need patches, that it was just an idea in his mind.

"It's pointless," Blue said. "You could tell him a hundred times and it wouldn't do any good."

"Then we'll tell him *two* hundred times, or however many times it takes!" answered Dr Grey.

Another patient complained that her medication was making her feel sick. Again Blue tried to bully the patient and again Dr Grey overruled her. After listening to the patient's story Dr Grey told Blue to reduce the medication a little.

"But why?" Blue wanted to know. "This one's always complaining about medication."

"All the more reason to do something about it."

"It'll just make her more troublesome!"

"People *behave* badly because they *feel* badly within themselves. The best way to improve behaviour is to take away some of the bad feelings." Dr Grey was addressing the whole meeting as well as Blue. You'd never heard a doctor saying things like this before. Always before it was as if psychiatry was a private mystery that belonged to the staff and which patients weren't entitled to know about. You realised in those few minutes that something very important was happening, and that it could change the whole situation for patients who were able to grasp it. If, as a patient, you are able to hear the kinds of things the doctor tells the staff, you'll be able to judge whether the staff are acting in accordance. Blue and the other screws and nurses realise this too and they don't like it.

It seems Dr Grey sat in on Ward Meetings and Group Therapy sessions throughout the hospital and said the same things. His name is mud now amongst almost all the staff. They call him "The Idiot". The odd thing is that Blue acts as though the patients ought to despise Dr Grey as much as she does. She often jokes with you about "The Idiot's latest brainwave" or something. You grin and agree.

Now the strike is happening.

All the nursing staff are out, except for a few supervisors and one screw or nurse left in each ward as an "observer". The "observer" is supposed to give necessary medical care so that nobody will die and create bad publicity. The "observer" isn't allowed to give psychiatric medication, only medical stuff like insulin, so you are free of the nuisance of having to spit your tablet down the sink. You've been watching other inmates to see how much madder they get without their medication. You can't see much difference.

The pantrymaids are out "in sympathy". The dixies of food are still being delivered from the main kitchen, so you and Con Pappas take over the pantry and keep the meals going. It's wonderfully peaceful at mealtimes now, without the shouting and abuse, though the "observer" nurse appears to feel that if the meals are being kept up the shouting and abuse should be kept up as well. You are dishing lunches across the servery. Christine waddles in a few minutes late and the "observer" yells that she can bloodywell go without so she'll learn to liven her bloody self up in future. It's intolerable. You push a meal across to Christine and she stares at it, her little fat chin wobbling with distress.

"Have your lunch, Christine," you say.

"I said she can go without!"

"Have your lunch, Christine."

"Did you hear what I said?"

"Take it, Christine. It's okay."

The room has gone very quiet. The "observer" is staring bug-eyed at you. Maybe she'll dash the plate on the floor or something. If so you'll dish up another. If this was a male screw he'd probably try a bit of knuckle at this stage. That'd be awkward. More importantly, it'd obscure the lesson of what is happening. The lesson is that bullying and abuse don't work without the whole apparatus of shock and punishment and Negative Reinforcement. The Apparatus has only been stopped for three days—after eighty years—and already this nurse has reverted to a puffed-up bag of nothing.

"Oh, have your bloody lunch!" she yells at Christine, then stalks out.

Later a supervisor comes round. The supervisors have been told by the union to stay on duty, for humanitarian reasons.

"If it was up to me I'd be out with the rest!" he tells you fiercely. He sees you are washing the dixies. "You doin' the pantry work here?"

"Just the necessaries," you say.

"Dishin' up meals?"

"That's right."

"A lotta people are feelin' pretty savage about anyone who helps undermine this strike action."

"I imagine so," you say. You aren't sure whether you are being threatened. This supervisor was already steamed-up when he came in, perhaps from the strain of his humanitarian role, and may just be cranky.

"And you're just doin' the necessaries?"

"That's all."

"Mmmm," he grunts, then walks around the pantry, examining it. He's looking at the floor to see if it's been mopped lately. Con Pappas starts to come in the other door with mop and bucket. You motion him away.

"Alright then," grunts the supervisor. He goes out.

Nothing much happens in REHAB during the strike. Cecil collapses with an asthma attack and the "observer"—a different one—agrees to phone for a doctor. "The German" comes and attends to him. All the doctors are working long hours in the geriatric and retard wards. "The German" walks through the dayroom on her way out.

"Iss everyvun heppy?" she calls.

"Happy as fuckin' Larry, Doc!" bawls Syd Hicks. Syd is getting frisky now without his Largactil. He's wearing only a singlet and a sock.

"Ach, I tink you are *too* heppy, eh?"

"Friggin' oath, Doc!"

"The German" wags a finger at him and goes out. It's hard work just keeping the geriatrics alive, so Syd Hicks being too happy hardly matters.

Mr Trowbridge is keeping OT open. You go a couple of times but Mr Trowbridge tells you you might as well stay and look after your ward and keep the meals going. The union is talking about having a strike over Mr Trowbridge as soon as the strike over Dr Grey is finished.

It ends after four days and the screws and nurses and pantrymaids come back. You are curious to see whether they keep a bit quiet for a day or so, or even for a few hours. They don't. If anything they are more swaggering than ever. Of course they've no reason not to be. The Apparatus is back in action.

And they've heard all about the episode of Christine's lunch. Blue jokes with you about it. It's okay. You and Blue understand each other.

14

Con Pappas has begun to change from the hangdog bloke you knew in MAX. He has combed his greying hair back in a wave and has grown a moustache which he trims carefully each morning. And he's got some new clothes, or maybe they are ones he's had in his suitcase for a few years. The yellow crocodile shoes attract a lot of attention. Con Pappas spends all his spare time trying to socialise with women inmates. You see him, with his wave and moustache and crocodile shoes, trying to be smooth and charming in a Greek sort of way. He's always escorting someone to the canteen for a soft drink, except when his withdrawals have been stopped for Negative Reinforcement. That's happening more often now. He can't understand why.

You try to talk to him.

"Listen mate, you'd better pull your horns in a bit."

"What means this?"

"It means watch out."

"I do nothing wrong."

"That's not the point. You're making yourself conspicuous. Those shoes, for instance."

Con Pappas looks offended.

"I'm not criticising them," you add hastily. "But Blue only needs some little thing to start her off."

But he doesn't get your drift.

It builds gradually, with Blue making remarks about the "two-bit Casanova". Other staff take it up and soon everybody's aware that Con Pappas is a bit of a sex maniac. You are in the dayroom, listening to the night-screw tell how he fucked two girls in the carpark at a disco last night. The screw notices Con Pappas sitting beside a female patient on the other side of the room.

"Hey, Casanova!" he calls. "You tryin' to get yer end in again?"

Con Pappas ought to make a joke of it. He should answer: "You're just jealous of my good looks," or something like that. But he probably doesn't understand a slang phrase like "get your end in", so he grins back sheepishly, to show he appreciates the humour—whatever it is—and says nothing.

"Shifty bastard," mutters the screw. He goes on with the story of the double fuck in the carpark. After a while he notices that Con Pappas and the woman patient are gone from their places.

"Hey, where's Casanova?" he yells.

"He's behind the partition," Christine says in her prim little voice.

"Come outa there, lover-boy," yells the screw. "I want ya where I can see ya."

You can imagine Con Pappas grinning sheepishly to his girlfriend and the other patients behind the partition. Showing he appreciates the humour. The screw goes on with the double fuck story and then about how he smashed a bottle over some bloke's head in a brawl inside the disco.

The radio is turned up loud behind the partition. It makes it hard to hear the TV and the fuck and brawl stories.

"Stop yer bloody racket, Pappas!" yells the screw. There are half a dozen patients behind the partition, but the screw has Con Pappas firmly in his mind. The radio goes low, then loud again. Some idiot's fiddling with it. Probably Syd Hicks. But Syd Hicks isn't in the screw's mind just now. The screw gets up and goes over.

"I told you before to come outa there!" you hear him telling Con Pappas. Con Pappas comes out, half-grinning, trying to appreciate the humour again.

"D'you reckon it's a bloody joke?" snaps the screw. "Alright then, you can get to bed!"

Con Pappas starts to say something in his soft-voiced, polite way.

"Don't argue the bloody point with me!" says the screw.

Con Pappas realises the humour—whatever it was—is over and he doesn't want trouble. He begins to say a last word to his girlfriend and takes a step towards her: but the step is in the opposite direction from bed. The screw grabs him and Con Pappas puts his arm up in surprise. This screw is a terrific disco brawler so he can handle the situation okay. He bends Con

Pappas's arm up his back and marches him from the room and up the stairs. Then he goes to write it all in the report book:

Sexually molesting a female patient.

Disruptive behaviour.

Abuse of ward property.

Disobedience.

Attempted assault of a staff member.

Blue will read the report in the morning but she won't be surprised. She saw this coming. Something beyond mere training and experience enables her to sense troublemakers even before they've made any. She's gifted that way.

You have invented a name for the process that is happening to Con Pappas—the Snowball. It begins with something trivial and gathers its own momentum. The Snowball is happening to different patients in various wards all the time, but it doesn't always go on rolling. If nobody's deliberately pushing it it can slow, then stop. This time it keeps rolling. The conditions are perfect for it. Con Pappas is perfect for it.

Con Pappas's misbehaviour is the main topic in Ward Meetings now, especially his sexual aggressions. Some female patients have realised how much better Blue treats them if they can report being "bothered" by Con Pappas. Elsie Haggart is "bothered" an awful lot. She and Blue will be bosom pals if the "bothering" keeps up. Christine hasn't been "bothered" herself, that would be too incredible, but she has her fat little eyes and her notebook and is always good for an eyewitness account: "I saw him interfering with Denise Williams ..."

"Is this true, Denise?" Blue demands.

Denise Williams looks vague.

"They went to the canteen together!" says Christine.

Denise Williams is trying to think. Maybe it was last Friday when she and Con Pappas happened to be walking on the same part of the road in the same direction.

"Did you agree to go to the canteen with him?"

"No."

"So he forced himself on you?"

"I went by myself," stutters Denise Williams.

"They were together!"

"Did you or did you not encourage him, Denise?"

"No," mumbles Denise Williams. She hardly knows what she is alleged to have done, or when, or with whom. It's best to just deny everything.

Blue turns to Con Pappas.

"Well, what have you got to say for yourself?"

"I do nothing wrong. I just go for walk."

"We all know what kind of walks *you* go for!"

"I no understand," says Con Pappas in his soft way. This always provokes Blue.

"You bloodywell understand alright!"

But it doesn't matter whether he understands or not. The Snowball goes on just the same. Con Pappas is on heavy medication now. The calisthenics are part of the Snowball too. Because of the medication he can't do movements as briskly as the watching screws and nurses want. They jeer: "Step it up, Casanova!" or "Hey, lover boy, you savin' yer energy for yer shaggin'?" Or they'll pretend he's done one less knee-bend than the others and will make him do ten extra to make up. So Con Pappas gets a reputation for shirking at calisthenics and the screws and nurses jeer harder each morning and the shirking reputation builds up until Con Pappas is as well known for his laziness as for his sex urge.

He doesn't wear the yellow crocodile shoes any more, nor the wave in his hair, nor the moustache; and he doesn't try to be smooth and charming with female patients. He's hangdog again, the way he was in MAX. Blue has noticed the change. She discusses it with Dr Muckerjee in the Ward Meeting.

"I'm concerned about Con Pappas, Doctor. He used to take a pride in his appearance and was socialising quite well. I really felt he was improving, but lately he seems to have relapsed into depression."

Dr Muckerjee nods. He's noticed it too.

"Is anything worrying you, Con?" Blue asks.

Con Pappas doesn't respond at once. He's on heavy medication and can't concentrate too well.

Dr Muckerjee nods. The patient is very withdrawn.

"I asked if anything's the matter, Con," Blue says.

"No," replies Con Pappas. The word comes out slurred because the medication makes it hard for him to control his tongue.

Dr Muckerjee nods. The patient lacks insight.

It is Tuesday morning. Con Pappas is being helped up the stairs to the little room where patients wait their turn for electroshock. He is very upset. He's crying. The screw is sympathetic and is urging Con Pappas up each step and telling him it's only a little way further to the room. This screw is a decent chap. Some screws would get impatient, but this one understands that inmates are victims of mental illness and need treatment. You go past and down to OT.

When you come back at lunchtime there is a stir in the ward. Christine tells you all about it. Con Pappas ran from the little room when the screw's back was turned, then fled from the ward. Some staff have driven around the grounds in cars but saw no sign of him. They think he's in the bush, planted somewhere nearby. Con Pappas isn't the type to make a real escape, and anyway he'd be too distraught to do the careful thinking he'd need to do. He's just holed up somewhere close, probably just wishing he was dead. On your way back from OT in the evening you see screws beating the bush along the lake on the far side of Glory Road. You join them and are there when Con Pappas is dragged from a swampy thicket. He struggles a bit and the screws get slime on their uniforms. They were treating the whole thing as a joke before, but that slime annoys them, especially a screw who's called "Bull" because of his big shoulders and big bull head. Bull bends Con Pappas's arm and marches him along, and when Con Pappas stumbles Bull lifts him up by the bent arm and Con Pappas groans with pain. Con Pappas only glances at you once but the glance makes you feel like Judas or something. It isn't fair. You're the one who warned him at the start about those crocodile shoes.

Con Pappas is a vegetable after eight shocks. He can't talk or understand or feed himself or use the lavatory. The only good thing about it is that Blue can't do anything more to him. Then the shocks are finished and after a week or so Con Pappas begins to be himself again, though he's still vague and clumsy and a bit helpless. He's a nuisance to the pantrymaids because he takes too long over his meals and they have to yell at him and threaten him even more than usual to show they aren't fooled by his act. You are washing the dixies, trying to block out the yelling. Bull is taking the medication tray around. He hands Con Pappas a little glass of syrup medication and Con Pappas spills it.

"Ahhh, bloody hell!" grunts Bull.

"He did it deliberate!" shouts a pantrymaid.

"Just watch yourself, sport," says Bull to Con Pappas.

"Make him clean it up!" shouts the pantrymaid.

"Yeah, go on. Clean it up," says Bull.

Con Pappas just sits looking vaguely from Bull to the pantrymaid and back again.

"Look at him!" cries the pantrymaid. "He thinks he can get away with murder!"

Bull is getting stirred. It'd be a reflection on himself if Con Pappas gets away with murder.

"I told you to clean it up!" he says, pulling Con Pappas from his seat. "Get a cloth and clean it up!" He pushes Con Pappas towards the servery where the cloths are. Con Pappas stands staring vaguely back at him. Bull is fully stirred now. He pushes Con Pappas harder so that he falls against the servery and a dixie of custard crashes to the floor. Bull wrestles a headlock on to Con Pappas and the two of them lurch and slide together in the spilt custard, then Bull drags Con Pappas from the room. It will all go in the report book:

Refusing medication.

Running amok in the dining room.

Attempted assault of a staff member.

The Snowball has begun again for Con Pappas. You wonder what happens after the Snowball has occurred over and over for a few years. A lobotomy?

A few minutes later you go to the Charge's office for some reason. Bull has Con Pappas in there. Blue is at the desk and a young nurse named Kean is behind her. Bull has a lock on Con Pappas's neck and is forcing his head back and trying to pour medication into his mouth. You stop in the doorway. Con Pappas is making choking noises and coughs the syrup out. Bull gives an exaggerated sigh, as though to indicate that this would exhaust even a saint's patience. He braces Con Pappas with one big arm, positions him, then punches him in the face. It makes a meaty sound.

Your impulse to interfere lasts only a moment. There's nothing you can do. The best thing is to take note of everything, fix it in your mind. Con Pappas's knees have buckled and there is blood down his shirt. Bull lowers him into a chair and begins wiping his big fist calmly, the way a workman would clean an implement after use.

Bull hasn't noticed you in the doorway. Blue has. You and Blue are looking into each other's eyes and the dare in Blue's eyes is louder than words: "Well, what are you going to do about it?"

You go to the verandah and pace up and down. Your stomach feels watery. You don't have to do anything. It doesn't concern you. What does a punch matter? Con Pappas has had worse done to him than that. And if you reported this it'd only be your word against the staff's. And *who* would you report it to? And how would you survive afterwards? No, there isn't a single good reason to risk yourself.

Except the dare in Blue's eyes.

Dr Grey isn't at his office in the Administration block. You go to his house but he isn't there either. You walk along the lake shore, seething. Dr Grey is the only one you trust and you'd need to tell him while the event is still fresh or there won't be any point. You are passing the canteen and you see "The German" come out and get into her car. Against your instinct you speak to her. She says casually that she'll look into the matter, then drives off. You wander back along by the water, feeling you've made a dreadful error and cursing Dr Grey for not being here.

When you return to REHAB you learn that "The German" has already been. It seems she dropped by on some routine errand and just happened to notice Con Pappas's injured face. She asked some questions and went away. Blue and Bull and a couple more are talking in the corridor and as you pass them you fancy that Blue gives you a long, calculating glance. But maybe it's just your guilty conscience.

Nothing happens for a week or so. You think it has blown over. Then you are called to the Medical Superintendent's office. A secretary has a notebook poised and a senior supervisor is sitting in a corner. Dr Grey tells you "The German" has made a report on certain injuries sustained by Mr Pappas and that he now requires a statement from you.

Did you, on such and such a date, make certain allegations?
Yes.
What were they?
You tell him.
What basis did you have for making them?
You tell him.
Later we get into detail:
Where were you in relation to other persons in the room?
You tell him.
Was the alleged blow struck with an open hand or closed fist?
You tell him.
And then the end:
Is this statement true and correct?
Yes.
Do you wish to add anything?
No.

Dr Grey shows you out a back door. You know Blue and Bull and Nurse Kean are in the building because you passed them on the way in. We are all making statements and the back door is to prevent collusion or intimidation. What you need is a back door right out of this hospital.

It's strange. You aren't sure what you expected—perhaps that the Apparatus would begin crushing you immediately, that you'd be shocked and medicated within a week. But nothing happens.

You go on washing dixies and leading the calisthenics and reporting on ward chores in the meetings. The staff speak to you when necessary and answer you when necessary and ignore you the rest of the time.

Bull ignores you especially. He doesn't even seem to see you any more. A couple of times he's come towards you in the corridor as though you weren't there and if you hadn't been careful he would have knocked you against the wall. Once or twice he has passed your chair and if you hadn't leant away quickly his big elbow would have hit the side of your head.

"I doubt he'd try anything too blatant," says Mr Trowbridge. "He's in enough trouble already." Mr Trowbridge is on your side. He hasn't felt much solidarity with his fellow staff since the strike. But you think he's exaggerating the trouble Bull is in.

"Surely it'll all blow over soon," you suggest.

"Not at all," says Mr Trowbridge. "Bull is to be officially charged."

"Fair dinkum?"

"Yes. Nurse Kean corroborated your story."

Bull has been suspended until the official hearing, so you don't see him. You don't see Nurse Kean either. She has resigned and gone to a job in the city and can't be contacted.

On the day of the hearing you are called to Administration and met by a man who says he's from the Crown Solicitor's department. He's prosecuting. He wants to clarify some points in your statement. Then he tells you to wait and you'll be called. He turns to go into the big room where the hearing is.

"What are the chances?" you ask him.

"Without Nurse Kean, not a cat in hell's."

The big room is set up like a court, with someone who looks like a magistrate behind a table raised at one end. Bull and his lawyer are at another table on one side of the room and the Crown Solicitor's man is across from them. A single chair is in the middle. There are eight or nine other people in the room. As you enter you see Dr Grey giving you a nod of encouragement. You are handed a Bible and told to repeat an oath. That seems odd, somehow. You half-think to remind them you are only a patient, in case the oath is a mistake. You sit in the chair in the centre and the Crown Solicitor's man asks you some questions. He reacts to your answers as though they are very good and helpful answers. Then Bull's lawyer takes over and he doesn't seem to feel your answers are good and helpful at all. He's been hired by the union and is dry and thin with a dry, thin voice. He asks you about your exact angle of vision when the alleged assault happened. He suggests you couldn't have seen the alleged blow struck because Bull's shoulder would have been in the way. Then he asks about your general attitude towards the staff.

"Do you get on well with them?"

"Reasonably well," you say.

"Only 'reasonably'?"

"I mean quite well."

"Why qualify it with 'reasonably'?"

"I mean I go my way and they go theirs." You realise your mistake at once.

"I see," says the dry, thin voice. "You go your own way."

"To a degree."

"And I suppose you have your own ideas about things?" The dry, thin voice puts an emphasis on "ideas". You know what he means by "ideas".

"To an extent," you say.

You are nervous now. You have a nagging thought that your fly might be undone. You're wearing old hospital pants with the fly held by a safety pin. You don't dare glance down so you lean forward uncomfortably to hide it. Then you think how peculiar you must look, crouching forward. You fluff the answers to a couple of questions and get more nervous than ever. When the dry, thin man is finished with you you slink from the room. Bull watches you go, a tiny smile on his lips. You were beginning to feel sorry for Bull. You've been on trial yourself and you know how it feels, but Bull·doesn't need your sympathy. He's more at home in that room, among those men in expensive suits, than you could ever be.

***

Bull is cleared. It doesn't matter. Nothing would be gained by him getting the sack. In a sense it would even be unfair, since what he does to people with his big fist is trivial against what Blue and her sort do to them with the Apparatus. And there aren't any official hearings about that. No, Blue would never be so crude and silly as to punch anyone in the face.

And yet you did vaguely imagine that reporting the assault would alter something. You weren't sure what. Certainly not the system, but *something*. It was a symbolic act, a moral protest, a case of the worm turning, and such things are supposed to have a power. Maybe you just thought it would make you feel better. In any case you were wrong. The routine in REHAB is back to normal and a turning worm is still a worm.

The main thing now is to avoid trouble, to be a model inmate and postpone as long as possible any episode that might begin the Snowball for you. Anything could start it and the staff have lots of time. You'll be here for years yet.

We are in the Ward Meeting. You've been a model patient for what seems like a long time and you've kept the Snowball from starting. It's easy being a model patient when you're scared of the Apparatus. You learn to put off petty resentments. Why *shouldn't* we be raved at in the dining room? Fourteen minutes is far too long to dawdle over a meal. It amounts to sheer victimisation of the pantrymaids! And so what if the Skin Man was battered senseless by the night-screw? Silly old coot asked for it, interrupting the screw's favourite TV show! And Blue's new scheme of mass reprisal is quite sound when you consider it. If someone forgets to wash up the morning tea things, everyone goes without morning tea next day. The staff aren't trained in psychology for nothing! Not only do you feel all these things are quite proper, you simultaneously understand that they aren't happening. The battering of the Skin Man didn't happen. If he has some bruises, well—the silly old fool's always falling over! You once had the notion that Bull bashed Con Pappas. Just shows how one can lose contact with reality! Lately Blue has resumed her interest in Con Pappas's welfare and he's been receiving some excellent new medication. Tomorrow he was to have the benefit of more electrical therapy.

Alas, he won't be here for it. This morning he broke open a locked razor and began cutting his throat. He's in the surgical ward now and may live.

Blue begins the Ward Meeting with a word about Con Pappas, then mutters to Wanda that we need sharper razors. They grin together.

"Why did he do it?" asks Christine. She hasn't the faintest.

"He was very disturbed," Blue explains.

"Oh, I wouldn't say that," you say. "Surely it showed an advance of insight?"

The staff all turn to look at you.

"What do you mean, Len?" asks Blue, inviting you to commit yourself further.

"He finally came to see the value of 'Negative Reinforcement' and wanted to give himself the ultimate form of it. You should be proud of him."

Blue regards you with pursed lips. She knew you'd drop the model patient act sometime and that she could begin to nail you.

The meeting goes on to other matters. The inmates are shirking calisthenics. Reprisals are threatened. Blue decides to test you, in case what you said before was just an isolated outburst.

"What do you suggest, Len?"

"Do what you like," you tell her. "I won't take part in calisthenics any more. Not while they're conducted by abuse, threats and mockery."

"I see," Blue murmurs. Yes, you've definitely dropped the model patient act and by the sound of it you'll be ridiculously easy to nail. What you've already said is evidence of persecution feelings. Within ten minutes there will be a fresh entry in the report book. Tomorrow morning when you refuse calisthenics the Snowball will begin to roll in earnest and within a few weeks it will have crushed you.

You are very frightened.

15

The letter comes the same afternoon. You open it and read it and you feel nothing at first but shame. You had almost lost faith. You had almost thrown away the only power you have. The power doesn't even belong to you really, you just have a slight use of it, a tiny candle flame of it, and you should have understood your duty better. Your duty isn't to go down in a forlorn gesture but to keep the candle flame alive at any cost.

Next morning you lead the calisthenics, cheerfully, in the cool sunshine. Screws and nurses mock us as usual. They have a special smirk for you. They think you've knuckled under again. Blue comes from the office to watch. You do extra knee-bends and jump higher than anyone else and you run on the spot quicker than you've ever done. What an abject worm you must appear.

In your pocket the heavy embossed paper that says you have won the National Poetry Prize. Sam Lister must have entered your poem.

The Medical Superintendent comes after breakfast with a copy of a big city newspaper and there's a bit on the front page about your Prize. Dr Grey shakes your hand and congratulates you. So does Blue, her face flushed with whatever she's feeling now. Screws and nurses crowd around to read the news. They can't believe it. Dr Grey says he's already had phone calls from reporters wanting interviews.

"I've told them it's entirely your decision."

Blue looks pained.

"Oh, I'm prepared to talk to them," you say.

Blue looks very pained.

Breakfast is delicious and the pantrymaids seem quieter than usual. They hardly raise their voices at all. Only dour old Mrs Fibbitson behaves exactly as normal. Good old stick! You go to OT and Janice and Cheryl give you a hug and a kiss. You think how once the idea of a hug and kiss from Cheryl was like a mad fever in you. You are normal now, cured of all fevers. Mr Trowbridge seems puzzled, probably figuring whether your prize poem amounts to a real job of Work. He decides it probably does and beams.

"Can I have your autograph?" cries Janice, pretending to offer a pen and book.

"Is your pen clean?" you ask, pretending to hesitate.

That day you do two phone interviews on radio, and a reporter comes for an article. Next day there's another radio interview and a reporter and photographer arrive from a big magazine. Of course the publicity is mostly vulgar and stupid—they don't care about poetry, it's just that you being a mental patient makes a good story. You talk to the reporters calmly, responsibly. You mustn't overplay it. Blue and her sort expect you to make wild accusations and slander the hospital. That would embarrass them but it'd also allow them to counterattack and show you up as deluded, persecuted, vindictive. You must play it cool, and keep the advantage.

On the third day a crew comes from a national TV news programme. They film a long interview by stages at different spots around the hospital. We even go to MAX and you stand again in the vegetable garden beneath the high wall. It seems a hundred years ago that you were here. The men are up on the verandah with their faces pressed against the wire mesh.

Someone yells "You bloody bewdy!" It's Bill Greene. He makes a kind of victory gesture with his arm and fist. You wave back. You try to pick out Ray Hoad's face but you can't see him. It doesn't matter. Suddenly it doesn't seem a hundred years ago. It seems now and for ever. You're a MAX man and glad of it!

Later the camera truck stops across the road from REHAB. We're getting a long shot of the entrance with the big words painted above. Blue comes out the door. She hasn't noticed the truck. She walks a little way, then freezes. A TV camera is pointed right at her. She can probably hear the faint whirr of it. She unfreezes, looks desperately around her, then *runs* back inside.

She *runs*!

***

Hundreds of ducks are rising into the evening sky, gathering into the salt air above the lake, making a soft swish of wings over Elsie Haggart's drowning place. You'll be seeing these ducks for years yet. Maybe you'll be released one day but it doesn't seem very important. Your victory will stand, whatever happens. The victory can't change anything directly: it won't necessarily stop the Apparatus crushing you, nor heal Con Pappas's slashed throat, nor help Ray Hoad who hanged himself in MAX today, but that isn't the point.

You watch the ducks go over, each one frail and separate within the dark mass, and you wonder what you really feel about the hospital. Right now it seems very beautiful. The thought comes that the beauty could not be so much if it weren't for the pain underneath.

No, you can't hate this place.